CYRILS
LOTTERY OF LIFE

CYRIL'S
LOTTERY OF LIFE

A hilarious tale of a small-town
English lawyer's quirky cases,
mystery & skullduggery

By

ALAN SHATTER

HERBITSHIRE PRESS

Published by Herbitshire Press in association with
Brown Dog Books and The Self-Publishing Partnership Ltd,
10b Greenway Farm, Bath Rd, Wick, nr. Bath BS30 5RL

herbitshirepress.com
Email: office@herbitshirepress.com

www.selfpublishingpartnership.co.uk

ISBN printed book: 978-1-83952-694-7
ISBN e-book: 978-1-83952-695-4

Cover design by Andrew Prescott
Internal design by Tim Jollands

Printed and bound in the UK

This book is printed on FSC® certified paper

ALAN SHATTER lives most of the time in Dublin, Ireland, with his wife Carol. For some time each year they live in Marco Island, Florida. He is a retired Irish politician, a former Irish minister for Justice, Equality and Defence, a political commentator, lawyer and author. He is the author over three decades of four major books on Irish family law that substantially contributed to its modernisation and reform. He is also the author of *Family Planning Irish Style* (1979), a satire on past Irish family planning laws, and *Laura* (Poolbeg, 1989), a best-selling novel that told the story of the heart-rending conflict over a child between the child's unmarried birth mother and potential adopters. His two most recent best-selling books are biographies, *Life is a Funny Business* (Poolbeg, 2017) and *Frenzy & Betrayal* (Merrion Press, 2019). In this, his first comedic novel, he utilises his thirty-five years of surreal experiences as a practising family lawyer to create an unforgettable group of quirky and idiosyncratic characters and uses their trials and tribulations as a vehicle for his very distinctive humour. He was recently quoted saying that 'Throughout my life I have spent far too much time immersed in the serious stuff trying to save the world. Knowing that life can be both funny and absurd I am now focused on having some fun, celebrating absurdity and spreading the laughter.'

For Carol,
who I am happy I can still make laugh.

Cyril's Lottery of Life

*CYRIL BRAITHWAITE

Former refuse collector, plumber and car salesman. Now practising as a solicitor in Oxton Town in the County of Herbitshire, reluctantly specialising in cases with a sexual undertone.

*MIRANDA BRAITHWAITE (nee MARSHALL)

Cyril's wife and the daughter of Cyril's deceased partner and former boss, Michael Marshall. Addicted to TV soaps, serials and reality shows and about to expand her horizons.

ALOYSIUS BRAITHWAITE

The son neither Cyril nor Miranda expected.

MICHAEL MARSHALL

Father of Miranda and although deceased, believed by some to still be a practising partner in the solicitors' firm of Braithwaite, Marshal & Co. A pillar of the community whose life is dramatically affected by an 'M' fetish.

MARTHA MARSHALL

Michael's widow who never anticipated Michael's infidelity and dramatic departure from the world. She escapes her angst by daily sharing with Miranda her televisual experiences.

*BARTHOLOMEW BULL
Much harassed former partner of Michael Marshall, now the senior partner in Moore Bull & Co. Attempting to come to terms with the complexities of life while flexing his biceps.

*PAMELA BULL
Bartholomew's wife, whose world descends into chaos thanks to his majesty's postal service.

*ETHEL EDELWITZ
Cyril's secretary, receptionist and girl Friday. Besotted by Cyril, secretly committed to having his children and to his reconfiguration from Catholicism to Judaism both physically and religiously. Starting the process by serving Cyril a daily diet of heavy-duty kosher food with a cholesterol overload.

CINDY BRETSON
Bartholomew's secretary, who could have obtained better paid and more rewarding employment elsewhere. Dedicated to the daily sorting of Bartholomew's post and emails.

*JOSHUA SHOSHOWSKI
One of the least successful criminals ever born. Having shattered Cyril's ideals is a greater success as a private detective than as a member of the criminal fraternity.

*SHEILA ENDWHISTLE
An unhappily married wedding planner and sometime client of Cyril who accidentally meets a chief superintendent.

FRED ENDWHISTLE
Sheila's alleged loutish husband who might just be a victim of circumstance.

JOACHIM JOXUM
No longer the man he was before.

*****CHIEF SUPERINTENDENT CHARLES MORROW**
The leading and most dedicated police officer in Oxton Town. An accidental introduction to Sheila Endwhistle dramatically changes his private life and recreational pursuits.

DR NORMAN ZENDLOVE
Oxton Town's only psycho-sexual counsellor, famous internationally for specialising in alphabet phobias and fetishes. He has just published his seminal work Exploring the Letters M–T.

GEOFFREY BREWER
An accountant leading a sedate and boring existence until he has lunch in his local New York deli and meets a mysterious woman from Queens.

JOCELYN BREWER
Geoffrey's wife whose problems also start with his majesty's postal service.

HILDA HESSLEBERG
Geoffrey's daily deli lunchtime companion. A recent widow committed to twelve months' celibacy, arm wrestling and knitting.

JEMIMA HARDCASTLE
A bereaved daughter with a grave problem.

HELEN GRAVELAWN
The beneficiary of a valuable cemetery plot.

JOHNNY BLEAK
A cemetery manager who enjoys a good laugh at a funeral.

MARIUS MOUNTMARTIN
A professional tennis coach with a touch of French and a country cottage.

DOUGLAS BEECHCROFT
A financially secure bank manager of military pedigree whose quest for a less ordered and more stimulating life has a Caribbean dimension.

CHARMAINE BEECHCROFT (nee LLOYD)
St Lucian dynamo who recognises the value of a substantial bank balance, teaches aerobics reggae style and has a commanding personality.

DESIREE HONEYCOMB
An accident-prone unisex hairstylist with a knockout brush.

ELDON PETTIGREW
A client of both Desiree and Cyril who has a bad hair day.

LILY PODGE
The distressed wife of a traumatised member of Oxton's judiciary.

JUDGE GERARD PODGE
A divorce judge who behaves like a baby, wears nappies and enjoys his nightly bottle.

ALPHONSE SMILEY aka CHARLIE CHUCKLES
A clown who wants to be taken seriously.

THE RUBBER TREE (Ficus Elastica)
Overgrown Amazonian evergreen trapped in Cyril's office and condemned to being his father confessor.

THE SWISS CHEESE PLANT (Monstera Delicrosa)
A newcomer to Cyril's office. Hungry for popularity, conversation and sun deprived.

Ingredients of Ethel Edelwitz's Favourite Food

BREAD PUDDING A pudding made with bread, sultanas and sugar.

CHOPPED LIVER A sort of rough liver pate made with fried chicken livers, onions and oil, put through a blender and served with grated hard-boiled egg on top.

GEDHAMPTA CHICKEN Boiled chicken in a sort of casserole.

GEFILTE FISH Minced white fish, rolled into balls and boiled in a fish sauce.

HOT SALT BEEF Beef pickled with spices, a bit like pastrami but not quite, usually eaten in a huge bread roll with mustard, sauerkraut and pickles.

KNAIDLACH Boiled dumplings made of matzo meal, egg and oil usually eaten with chicken soup.

LATKES Potato fritters, deep fried.

LOCSHUN PUDDING A sweet dish of flat pasta, raisins, egg and sugar baked in the oven.

POTATO KUGEL Potato pudding baked in the oven, bit like a baked latke.

TZIMMES A stew made with potatoes, carrots, dried fruit and other root vegetables.

VURSHT A large savoury beef sausage full of fat, particularly good with fried eggs and French fries. A real heart stopper!

1

CYRIL BRAITHWAITE had status. He now not only had letters after his name but had a profession. He was no longer simply Cyril Braithwaite of Larkspur Grove, thirty-five years of age, three and a half years married, one son Aloysius aged three, four brothers, three sisters, five foot ten inches in height, dishevelled straight brown hair, brown eyes, average weight, former refuse collector, former trainee plumber and car salesman. He was now Cyril Braithwaite LLB, solicitor. He had finally made it.

The university night courses at Oxton University in Herbitshire had started seven years earlier. At first he thought he would do it all in four. After he had failed his first-year law exams he knew it would take longer. After he was responsible for Miranda, his twenty-three year-old girlfriend of six months and the daughter of the senior partner in Moore Marshall Bull and Co Solicitors, accidentally becoming pregnant due to his condom splitting, he feared he would not make it at all.

Miranda's determination to have their baby and Cyril's marriage to Miranda had changed everything. Michael Marshall's gratitude for them both agreeing to marry before the extended Marshall family and friends noticed Miranda's condition resulted in their wedding present of a small detached three-bedroom house in Larkspur Grove and an annuity of £150,000 a year to ensure Miranda continued to lead the luxurious lifestyle she had enjoyed as an unmarried, non-pregnant young Marshall. Selling clapped out cars to greedy bargain hunting car purchasers became a thing of Cyril's past and full-time studying had become a thing of Cyril's present. Now the studying was over and having completed his two years of training, a full-time job awaited Cyril as an assistant solicitor in his father-in-law's solicitors' firm.

From the moment it dawned on Cyril that his entering this world had been dependent on the accidental capacity of a spermatozoa to outswim its potential brothers and sisters in the fertilisation stakes, Cyril started to suspect life is something of a lottery. If he had then known that the spermatozoa responsible for his existence had been prematurely and unexpectedly launched into the world and that its launch had come as a surprise to his father, who at the vital moment was frantically but unsuccessfully attempting to take evasive action to abort lift off, his suspicion that he was the outcome of a game of chance would have hardened. If he had been told that the paternal premature launch on which his very existence depended had been a cause of disappointment to his mother (albeit one of many similar disappointments experienced by her in similar circumstances throughout her marriage to his father), which six weeks later caused considerable consternation when it finally dawned on her that she had got her calendar dates wrong, his suspicions would have been confirmed.

Fortunately or unfortunately, depending on how you look at it, although looking at it was never the prime cause of her problems as far as Cyril's mother was concerned, none of this was ever discussed over the family dinner table. It remained a private unacknowledged part of the Braithwaite family history.

Despite Cyril's blissful ignorance of his premature and accidental beginnings, he eventually recognised that if life is a lottery you cannot win unless you buy a ticket. Having dropped out of school at the age of sixteen, the need to buy the ticket dawned on him some twelve years later as he stood in the rain in a used car lot extolling the virtues of a nine-year-old heap of motorised junk that had already clocked up over 170,000 miles to a somewhat senile, cash carrying, slightly inebriated retired bank manager, oblivious to the risk of becoming a road casualty statistic.

Cyril by then had concluded that there is no grand design and that if he did not wish to spend the rest of his days on planet earth working in used car lots, no god would reach down from the heavens and redirect his life. He knew from practical experience that there is no one out there who simply gives you a hand and a leg up when one is needed. In the absence of other available helping hands, you have to use your own. He figured if life is a lottery he better buy his own winning ticket.

To Cyril a university night course in law was that ticket. The wheel of fortune turned full circle when family history repeated itself and his own accidentally launched spermatozoa hit bullseye with Miranda late one Saturday night in the alley behind Oxton Town's oddly named notorious premier night club, the Gyrating Chicken. This taught Cyril that life is not only a lottery but that even after purchasing a winning ticket unpredictable stuff can happen with unexpected consequences. What Cyril initially feared would result in a booby prize sentencing to used car lots for life, unexpectedly resulted in his hitting the jackpot. In the world of spermatozoa Cyril proved that without doubt he is his father's son!

2

SIX MONTHS AFTER Cyril qualified and took up the position of assistant solicitor to Michael Marshall more stuff happened and disaster struck. Unknown to Cyril or Miranda and, even more distressingly, unknown to Miranda's mother Martha, one Mary Belle Brown, who was Michael Marshall's thirty-seven-year-old, bright blue eyed, blond secretary, had been enthusiastically providing Michael with benefits in kind of an untaxable variety for over four years.

Known to be a generous man, Miranda's father's generosity extended to the portions of food he himself consumed on a daily basis. Although weighing in at 245 pounds from his epicurean indulgences, he was no slouch when it came to sex. Martha had once revealed to her golfing friends at the nineteenth hole in Oxton's local golf club during a largely liquid lunch that his appetite for sexual pleasure was as veracious as his consumption of food. She at no stage, however, suspected infidelity.

Martha's distress at discovering Michael's adulterous habits was compounded by the bizarre circumstances of the revelation and the shock and horror reported in the local and national tabloids. In the public interest and to ensure the entire population of the United Kingdom was fully informed of the cataclysmic event, various newspaper editors determined Michael Marshall's exploits worthy of unmissable front-page headlines in thick black print, seven inches long, the length of which was subsequently deemed extraordinarily appropriate by the few readers who went to the trouble of measuring the headlines. Thereafter, the story went viral on social media. However, it wasn't the incessant media coverage that most upset Martha but her failure to detect the obvious warning signals. She realised that she should have anticipated that Michael would have been unable to resist the temptations offered by a secretary whose first name began with an 'M'. It was Martha's name which had first attracted his attention and Michael had insisted that all of their children be christened with an 'M'. In addition to Miranda there was Melvyn, Maurice, Myles, Mervin, Mable, Melissa and Marigold. For Michael Marshall the letter 'M', being the thirteenth letter in the alphabet, had an unusual and irresistible attraction.

For Cyril it was the nature of the discovery that shocked most. Walking into his father-in-law's externally locked office through his own office's internal unlocked interconnecting door at the end of a difficult day spent in court, he was astonished to find a naked Mary Belle Brown, eyes wide open, arms outstretched above her head, hands tied, mouth taped, skin a slightly purple colour, lying immobile on top of Michael Marshall's desk. On top of her lay a similarly immobilised solicitor, underwear and trousers around his ankles and head buried between her generously proportioned breasts. There was no suggestion that Mary Belle Brown had been unlawfully coerced or pressured into her desk-top adventures, nor anything other than trim and healthy when she arrived in the office that morning, nor did anyone believe that Michael Marshal, solicitor, was into necrophilia. A joint interest in S&M

was suspected but unproven. The subsequent medical prognosis, the medics having carried out a detailed autopsy, was that his father-in-law had suffered a massive simultaneous coronary and orgasm. Which came first was initially the cause of some heated debate between the clinically qualified. Eventually, after considerable argument, in the interests of preserving medical harmony, those obliged to make a finding agreed on a draw. It was also concluded that having gone from the world as he was coming, Michael Marshal had by his vast bulk asphyxiated Mary Belle Brown, who after being sole witness to her boss's climactic departure from the legal profession was unable to escape from under his oversized remains or to call for help. Medical opinion was also somewhat confused as to whether Mary Belle had gone when she was coming or whether she had gone without coming at all. There was, however, no doubt that by the time Cyril found them they had both become 'the late departed' and the large black whip looking forlorn abandoned on the floor by the side of the desk had become a bereaved orphan.

The remaining partners in Moore Marshall Bull & Co within days of this unsettling and unexpected event hitting the nation's headlines decided for their own professional preservation that the time had arrived to totally end the Marshall connection, the departed Marshall's connection being viewed by one and all as the cause of the firm's embarrassment and massive public relations disaster. Cyril not only found himself out of a job but Miranda found herself without the financial support of her father's £150,000 annuity, the income to fund it having dramatically ended.

In the lottery of life Cyril felt his luck had again turned. The publicity derived from the subsequent inquest held three months later in which he had to describe in precise detail the positions in which he found the bodies and the exact location of their private parts diminished further his employment prospects. The inquest verdict on Mary Belle Brown was aptly described by the coroner as 'death by misadventure'. If his father-in-law had survived his late departed secretary's 'misadventure', Cyril announced to anyone who would listen he would have had him charged with manslaughter. A charge of murder, he concluded, would have been impossible as Mary Belle's unconventional demise could not be attributed to an unprovoked attack with an intention to kill. It was universally quietly acknowledged by the politically incorrect that Michael Marshall's terminally acrobatic endeavours must have been provoked by the selfishly stunning good looks of his once vivacious secretary, with whom he was having a secret affair, and by her parents' lack of insight in giving her a name starting with the thirteenth letter of the alphabet. What Mary Belle had seen in his father-in-law other than an oversized belly and a spectacularly shiny bald head remained an unresolved mystery, although rumour had it that she may also have had an 'M' fetish. If so, Cyril had to acknowledge that she would have found Michael Marshall's double 'M's irresistible.

3

SEVEN MONTHS AFTER his discovery of the copulating cadavers, Cyril sat in his favourite armchair in the lounge room of his Larkspur Grove home situated in Oxton's stockbroker and legal belt examining the huge increase in his and Miranda's joint overdraft displayed in thick red print on the Midland Bank couriered copy account just delivered. It was accompanied by a letter signed by Douglas Beechcroft, the manager of the bank's local branch, demanding the overdraft be rapidly reduced. Prior to the courier's arrival, he had been reflecting on the dramatic passing of his father-in-law and on the discomfort of the unfortunate ambulance attendants who had speedily responded to his emergency call. For ten minutes they had struggled to prise the bodies apart to enable each of the late departed, at the end of their life journey, to descend the lift of Moore Marshall Bull & Co (now renamed Moore Bull & Co) on individual stretchers so that the circumstances of their demise would not be exhibited to all and sundry and some of their dignity preserved. The onset of rigor mortis had not made their task easy.

The unexpected couriered communication from the bank forced Cyril to focus on more immediate problems and he swiftly acknowledged to himself that there was again a need to take things into his own hands and act decisively. Two nights earlier he had inconsiderately remarked to Miranda that if her late father had adhered to Cyril's philosophy of self-service none of the current bother would have happened. After this unfortunately tactless comment she had temporarily left their bed and moved into the spare bedroom, remarking that if that was the way he felt, he could now apply his philosophy of life to finish off what they had just started.

Cyril now resolved that despite his inexperience he would open his own legal practice. He believed that he had no other option as it was clear that no firm of solicitors in Oxton would employ him for fear that clients would consult him to just satisfy a morbid curiosity to discover how a post coronary dead man could sustain an erection for two hours after all other bodily functions, including breathing, had ended. If any curious clients wanted to discuss Michael Marshall's death he was happy to do so and to satisfy their curiosity, provided they paid a sufficiently gratifying consultation fee in advance of any meeting; £400 a pop, Cyril reasoned, would provide the gratification required.

Two weeks later the firm of Braithwaite Marshall & Co opened its doors for business. To those not in the know who sought an appointment with Mr Marshall the telephonist would simply explain that 'he is no longer with us, but Mr Braithwaite would be happy to see you.' For the first few months a procession of Michael Marshall's former clients visited Cyril's office with a variety of spurious legal queries and problems just to get the lowdown on the real facts behind Michael Marshall's unexpected departure from the legal world. A vile rumour had circulated that although his father-in-law had suffered brain death by the time Cyril entered his office, the lower parts of his body were still vibrating. Not a man to spoil a good story, Cyril did nothing to dispel the rumour. Ambiguity became a close friend and clarity a mortal enemy. If potential clients wanted to discuss Michael Marshall's unexpected sexual prowess and acrobatics in both life and death at £400 a consultation, he would say nothing to disillusion them and undermine a solidifying myth.

To keep his records in order and to separate client's real legal issues from the spurious, the names and addresses of the curious were separately recorded electronically on Cyril's spanking new state-of-the-art computer programme under the acronym FILS, short for father-in-law/secretary. By now the whole concept of a father in something had taken on a new and decidedly specific meaning for Cyril. Nevertheless, he resisted the temptation to insert a comma after the 'F' and delete the dashes in the acronym realising he was in enough trouble with Miranda already. He had no wish to risk exacerbating matters should she unexpectedly call into the office to accidentally discover what even he acknowledged was a somewhat tasteless joke as a result of his having inadvertently left his laptop open on the FILS folder.

The publicity resulting from Michael Marshall's death and the matter-of-fact manner in which Cyril described events to the incredulous gathered in Oxton's coroners court resulted in a widespread public perception that Braithwaite Marshall & Co were the solicitors to consult about personal sexual problems and related issues with a legal overtone. It was obvious to all that there could be nothing happening in a person's private life nor anything they were doing with their private parts that could shock or unsettle Cyril after his exposure to the desk-top proclivities of human desire exhibited in his deceased father-in-law's office.

After twelve months of legal practice on his own Cyril reckoned that 95% of his real legal work was concerned with potential divorce and family separation cases. A treasure trove of human sexual endeavour and deviation had been described, documented and recorded in morbid detail in relation to husbands, wives, same sex spouses and cohabitees who were anxious to know the possible legal consequences of a spouse or partner discovering some of the illicit physical feats of human ingenuity in which they were secretly engaged. Few of those who sought his advice were actually seeking a divorce or separation. Most just sought assurances that they would not be taken totally to the cleaners if their extracurricular exploits were discovered by their unsuspecting and still trusting official conjugal partners. Over time, Cyril learnt that although he could not usually give the assurances they craved, it fortunately did not deter their enthusiasm for ongoing very personal extra curricular adventures. From Cyril's perspective this was definitely a positive as it held out the prospect of future more lucrative engagements.

4

CYRIL FREQUENTLY found himself in court. The first case in which Braithwaite Marshall & Co appeared proved to be a minor disaster, through no fault of Cyril.

Sheila Endwhistle of 21 Chester Ave, Oxton Town presented as a large, rotund woman, approximately 270 pounds in weight, five foot nine inches tall with a propensity to wear low-cut designer tops two sizes too small. Sitting opposite Cyril in his office she rested her large over-exposed size forty-two protrusions on the edge of his desk as she described various alleged assaults on her person by her allegedly vicious and demented husband. A divorce is what she wanted, she informed Cyril, as he struggled to retain a sympathetic expression and to keep his eyes firmly on the tip of her nose to maintain concentration. With some difficulty he retained his composure, when to prove her point Sheila suddenly leapt up in front of his desk and hosted her tent-like skirt up around her waist to reveal a deep purple patch on the top of her left thigh. Until that moment the raised tent had with remarkable efficiency covered the vast dimensions of her trunk-shaped legs. A millisecond later all pretence at composure disintegrated. Gripped by panic and drowned in a cold sweat Cyril ordered her to sit down. The raising of the tent had not merely revealed the bruise allegedly inflicted the night before by a brutal and unprovoked kick from Fred Endwhistle's left foot but had also revealed the unexpected sight of the most massive pair of red and yellow crotchless panties Cyril had ever set eyes on. Confirming to his newly acquired client that divorce papers alleging assault, cruelty and unreasonable conduct would within a matter of days be served on her unsuspecting husband, he bustled her out of the office and then drank a neat double whiskey to steady his nerves.

Sheila Endwhistle's subsequent visits to Cyril's office were conducted with more decorum than her first. At the start of her second visit, Cyril having expressed appropriate concern, firmly resisted a further display of alleged marital war wounds. Instead of checking them out himself, he ordered his uninhibited client to photograph any visible injuries and to visit her family doctor to enable him to record them and send a report to Cyril detailing their particulars. Cyril also wrote to her doctor confirming what he required and advising that he might be asked to give evidence in court.

In response to Sheila's court papers, Fred Endwhistle denied all allegations of assault and asserted that Sheila had been bedding ten percent of the entire male inhabitants of the local village of Mordick. Despite that, Fred said, he still loved her and wanted no divorce. Sheila protested her innocence and insisted Cyril file replying court papers describing Fred's 'perverted and false allegations' to be additional proof of the brute's heartless cruelty. She also demanded that Cyril include a complaint about Fred's bedtime flatulating habit.

Living up to the name of Endwhistle, she complained to Cyril that most nights he flatulated his way through the late-night television news while lying in bed and drinking a mug of hot chocolate accompanied by a large packet of Walkers cheese and onion crisps. Cyril fought back a look of incredulity when told she had threatened Fred with a visit from Oxton Council's lone anti-pollution officer to conduct an air pollution investigation in their bedroom in the hope he would have Fred jailed. She complained that the negligent bureaucrat had declined her request for a late-night home visit, protesting that he only worked from nine till five, explaining that the Conservative-controlled council, staggering on the brink of insolvency, would not sanction any late-night overtime. As Fred only flatulated at night she had been obliged to abandon this possible remedy to her problems and resort to divorce proceedings. Cyril learnt that the assaults about which she had first complained were to Sheila only a minor irritation upon her confessing she gave as good as she got. For her it was Fred's repetitive nocturnal hemorrhoidal expulsions that were the real problem.

'I am one of the busiest wedding planners in Oxton Town,' Sheila told Cyril. 'But when planning my own wedding I never anticipated I would end up married to one of the world's leading human producers of flatulent-created methane and that my bedroom would become a polluted ecological disaster area. Did you know, Mr Braithwaite, that humans on average emit one litre per day of flatulent gases?'

'Er, no I didn't,' replied Cyril.

'Well I reckon Fred nightly emits ten times that amount,' Sheila asserted. 'He is not only getting up my nose he is also making a unique very personal contribution to global warming.'

Denying his wife's 'foul allegation' in replying court papers Fred inexplicably once again asserted his love and admitted he had suffered gastric problems some two years earlier caused by Sheila going through her hot curry and garlic cooking phase. In response, when asked, Sheila mysteriously muttered, 'Endwhistle's the name and Endwhistle's the game,' and thereafter made no further mention of her husband's alleged polluting tendencies.

Six months after Sheila's first visit to his office and five consultations later Cyril was sitting opposite the entrance to Oxton's divorce county court waiting for the case of Endwhistle v Endwhistle to be called, his client located a safe distance away in a consultation room down the hall from the courtroom. As Cyril was reflecting on the vital components of the Endwhistle case he was unexpectedly joined by his client, who was clearly somewhat put out she had been kept waiting. She bitterly complained about His Honour insisting on first concluding the hearing of a divorce case carried over from the previous day before embarking on her 'much more important hearing'. After engaging in a few brief casual unpleasantries about her uncouth husband and imbecilic judges, Sheila Endwhistle suddenly fell strangely and unusually silent. All colour drained from her face as she stared open mouthed across the court hallway at a small man about five foot one inch tall who at that moment had entered the waiting area. He was accompanied by a solicitor Cyril recognised as representing her husband and two other much taller men, each obviously uncomfortable in the unfamiliar court surroundings.

Suspecting something was up but not sure of its exact dimensions or relevance to the impending court hearing, Cyril rapidly sought an explanation from his distraught client.

'The small one over there, he's my husband,' she told Cyril, who had expected a more ferocious looking example of the brutal male species considerably taller in stature. 'The other two men, the tall ones, are neighbours.'

'And why are they here?' Cyril quietly enquired.

'Well one night when Fred was away they called in to take me out for a drink and we spent a couple of hours together in the Pig and Whistle, our local pub. Then they walked me home,' Sheila explained.

Cyril wondered was he missing something vital. Confused by his client's obvious consternation, he sought more details of Sheila's night-time outing.

'They said they wouldn't tell him you all went out for a drink, is that it?' he tentatively enquired.

'Well not quite, they came in after walking me home and didn't leave till the following morning.'

Alarm bells ringing in his head and fear that Endwhistle v Endwhistle was about to be called Cyril plunged in, dropping all attempts at diplomacy.

'After they came into the house did you do anything with them?' he hurriedly asked.

'See the one over there, the one with the pink tie and the blue pinstripes, I'm afraid stuff happened, Mr Braithwaite,' she unblushingly responded.

'Exactly what stuff?' enquired Cyril, anxious to not jump to hastily inaccurate conclusions.

'We fucked upstairs in my bedroom,' she replied simply.

'Oh, I see. And what did the one in the beige suite do while you were... er... upstairs?' he timidly asked.

'Ah, Mr Braithwaite,' she replied without hesitation, 'we couldn't leave him alone, he came up to watch. In fact at one point he got so excited and turned on that he fell into the bed on top of me. I got the most dreadful purple bruise on my left thigh.'

At that very moment the court crier's voice echoed around the hallway as a surge of humanity exited from Oxton's divorce county court signalling the end of the previous day's case.

'Endwhistle v Endwhistle,' he called.

A few minutes later the judicial whistle blew and the hearing commenced but before a single piece of evidence had been given Cyril knew for Sheila Endwhistle the game was up. Due to the falsity of her court pleadings, Fred's professed unrequited love and express wish to reconcile, the divorce would be refused. Cyril's one small victory was in persuading His Honour Judge Gerard Podge to not forward the papers to prosecuting authorities to consider charging Sheila with perjury. He accepted Cyril's impassioned plea that it was in both parties' interests that he do nothing to undermine the possible restoration of marital bliss and harmony or that could damage Sheila's successful business reputation as a wedding planner.

5

A NUMBER OF LESS noteworthy divorce cases followed, interspersed with the occasional minor criminal matter. Cyril's social conscience and belief that many of life's petty criminals were merely the victims of society rather than its enemies was dealt a terminal blow when he represented one Joshua Shoshowski. Joshua was the thirty-two-year-old son of an unmarried waitress from Maidenhead and a sailor from Kraków in Poland whose forty hours of onshore leave in Liverpool was responsible for Joshua's conception and his mother's loss of that part of her physiology that coincided with the name of her town of origin. Joshua's beginnings confirmed to Cyril, in so far as confirmation was needed, that life was indeed a lottery. If Joshua's father had been granted shore leave in St Petersburg instead of Liverpool, Cyril reasoned, Joshua would not have been born nor become one of Cyril's clients.

Cyril defended Joshua against thirty-six criminal charges, all involving petty theft. To Cyril, Joshua was one of the most incompetent villains of all time. Explaining that his house-breaking activities had been motivated by a desire to provide a decent standard of living for his sick mother, who had thirty-three years earlier been ostracised by her family upon the discovery of her pregnancy, Joshua promised Cyril that if he kept him out of jail he would give up his life of crime. His mother, Joshua told Cyril, had been driven out of her family home to the shouts of her heartless, intemperate and semantically confused father that he would not allow a daughter of his to remain at home 'if she was up the pole'. Unknown to Joshua, who at that moment was a mere speck within his mother's internal universe and unknown to his mother, who only that day had learnt of her pregnant condition, the only Pole relevant to the family predicament was at that very moment on the open seas half way to Vladivostok, never to return.

Joshua's alleged offences included the larceny of fifteen car radios from random parked cars, twenty-five pairs of ladies' panties and thirty-two thongs from Lily's Lingerie Shop, thirty chickens from Nolan's, the butcher, and seventy-eight packets of black mint-flavoured condoms from a condom dispenser attached to the outside wall of Oxton's family planning clinic. The police had intercepted Joshua at 11.30 p.m. one night walking down Oxton High Street with a sack of pre-packaged frozen chickens wearing a thong-like mask over his face in a pathetic attempt to conceal his identity from the newly installed on-street security cameras. Some hours later, having been released on station bail, Joshua had been forced to call for help from a passing police car having impaled his right arm on the jagged edge of a car glass window he had broken. The car was parked around the corner from the police station. Putting his arm through the broken window to remove a briefcase thoughtlessly abandoned on the front passenger seat, he had failed to observe the glass remnant which cut through and stuck in a vein. He told Cyril, he believed it was a question of either seeking help and again being copped or pulling out his arm and bleeding to death. Opting for life and possible imprisonment instead of self-help and a permanent home underground, he chose the former, concluding he was too young to become a cemeterian.

Having been arrested for the second time that night, much to his surprise, Joshua was speedily released after the delivery of a stern warning about the fate awaiting him should he rob another car. The only reason the incident didn't increase the number of charges from thirty-six to thirty-seven, Cyril later discovered upon enquiry, was that fortuitously the car in question and the briefcase were the property of Chief Superintendent Charles Morrow who did not wish to reveal in evidence the briefcase's contents. It apparently contained not only two boxes of the black mint-flavoured condoms earlier impounded from Joshua and seven explicit pictorial magazines which exhibited a variety of male and female contortionists in physically mind-boggling poses but also, as advertised in two of the magazines, 'an adult-sized anatomically stunning and authentically lubricated blow-up doll with real human hair.'

The chief superintendent, being the most prominent and best-known member of the local constabulary, did not wish to have to explain under cross-examination the reason for the rather strange hoard in his personal Oxton Constabulary embossed briefcase. Chief Superintendent Morrow had logically concluded that if the general public learnt what he did when off duty with his prominent member he would become a laughing stock. For him there would be no tomorrow as a prominent chief superintendent.

Concluding that if Joshua had been the child of a happily married female bank official and male accountant he would not have led a life of crime and relying on his promise to reform, Cyril resolved to keep his client out of jail. Contacting the chief superintendent he informed him that his client wanted to make a clean breast of it and start his life over again. He was willing to plead guilty to all charges and save the expense of thirty-six separate trials on which Cyril would insist and avoid the impact they would have not only on local policing but also in clogging up the court system subject to one condition: the chief superintendent had to support Cyril's plea to the trial judge to not jail Joshua but instead to require him to make restitution for his crimes by undertaking community service. The initial dismissal with much laughter of this 'outrageous' proposal accompanied by a verbalised commitment to 'send Shoshowski away for ten years' disintegrated rapidly upon Cyril stating that in the absence of police cooperation his client would not only plead guilty to the thirty-six charges before the court but also to a thirty-seventh offence for which he had not as yet been charged.

Joshua, Cyril explained, wished to have a clean slate so that upon release from prison, whatever the sentence, he would not be vulnerable to any outstanding prosecution. This latter offence, said Cyril, involved the attempted larceny of a black briefcase from a parked car, the contents of which would have to be detailed in court together with the owner's identity. Two weeks later the chief superintendent's unusually impassioned plea on Joshua's behalf so impressed Judge Anthony Black in Criminal Court 4 that he announced that in his view society should give Joshua a chance. Instead of his being sentenced to imprisonment, the judge required that he undertake 240 hours of community service at five hours per week.

Having been embraced by Joshua, Cyril retired to the court cafeteria, treated himself to a skinny latte and a jam cream doughnut and reflected on his triumph. Half an hour later, standing around the corner from the court building, searching his jacket pocket for the electronic key to his car door, he noticed that the front passenger window of his car was broken in and his expensive satellite radio, speakers and music system were missing. On the roadway where the broken glass had fallen, there lay the familiar letterhead of Braithwaite Marshall and Co. Picking it up Cyril discovered a tea-stained letter addressed to one Joshua Shoshowski confirming that 'Mr Braithwaite will meet you outside Criminal Court 4 at 10.30 am' that morning. Clearly, Cyril's advice to Joshua that he should not rely on others but should go out into the world and do it for himself had been taken on board by his client as authorising his return to a life of crime. Realising that theories of self-help mean different things to different people, including chief superintendents, Cyril was never again troubled by a social conscious and lost all interest in criminal law.

6

E THEL EDELWITZ KEPT her long jet-black hair tied up in a
bun and wore heavy silver-framed glasses. Aged thirty-one,
five foot six inches in height, her most noticeable and prominent
physical feature was a large red pimple which had temporarily
appeared on the top of her nose. She was a methodical and
articulate telephonist and secretary who Cyril believed to be
the ideal employee. With Ethel around he had concluded there
was no possibility of him being tempted to emulate Michael
Marshall's unorthodox cardiac demise.

Cyril had first met Ethel in the former firm of Moore Marshall
Bull & Co where she had not only worked as his secretary but
had also introduced him to what she described as Jewish gourmet
cooking. Cyril's involuntary departure from the firm had resulted
in her redundancy and his feelings of guilt that his or more
correctly, his father-in-law's connection with the firm had forced
her to join the army of the jobless, resulted in his offering her the
position of telephonist, typist and office manager in Braithwaite
Marshall & Co. Her gratitude at his so speedily providing her with
alternative employment propelled her into a daily kosher cooking
fiesta in the small shared kitchen in the basement of their new
office building that posed a serious threat to Cyril's cholesterol
levels. Ethel believed it to be part of her daily duties to provide

Cyril with his lunch. 'Cyril Braithwaite,' she would tell anyone who would listen, 'is too important a man to eat sandwiches at lunchtime. What he needs, particularly during the winter, is a good solid meal.'

The emphasis was particularly on the solid. Latkes, lokshen pudding, potato kugel, bread pudding, hot salt beef, vursht, gefilte fish, knaidlach and chopped liver became part of Cyril's Jewish dietary vocabulary, all of them epicurean concepts alien to his Catholic background and life experience prior to his becoming a member of the legal profession.

As he and Ethel celebrated the first anniversary of the formation of Braithwaite Marshall & Co over a lunch of chicken soup and knaidlach, roast stuffed chicken and potato kugel followed by a dessert of bread pudding, it dawned on Cyril, who weighed one and a half stone more than a year earlier, that his secretarial cooked lunches probably posed as great a threat of an early coronary as his father-in-law's reckless desk-top adventures. As he fell asleep in an office armchair, the meal over, he resolved that prior to celebrating the firm's second anniversary he would become a vegetarian. He would, however, allow himself the occasional pub ham sandwich for which he had a strange and unusual craving.

* * *

Ethel idolised Cyril. She believed he had been badly treated by Michael Marshall's surviving partners. Cyril was not to blame for any goings on in the firm and she told anyone interested that it was unfair that Cyril's unexpected discovery of his father-in-law's illicit philandering resulted in each of them losing their job. She was determined that one day Braithwaite Marshall & Co would exact revenge for both her and Cyril's victimisation. For the time being her job was to be the perfect secretary, receptionist and girl Friday.

As well as filling the void created by his wife Miranda's lack of culinary skills, as Braithwaite Marshall & Co entered its second year, Ethel determined to protect Cyril from some of the madder or more prurient potential clients who sought a consultation without really being in need of legal advice or help. It was sometime later that Cyril realised there was an alarming reduction in the number of his consultations with new clients. Instead of his day being filled with phone calls and meetings, he had spare time on his hands and no outstanding work to complete. Unknown to Cyril a potential new client who first sought an appointment had to overcome an obstacle course erected by Ethel, who arbitrarily assumed responsibility for a preliminary assessment of their sanity and bone fides.

Ethel determining a phone caller's legal issue to be spurious did not mean that it was. Her deciding people to be crazy did not, of course, mean that they were. In fact, if many of the unsuspecting who phoned Cyril's office had realised that Ethel was recording their conversations, it would have confirmed to them the accuracy of the serious doubts they developed about Ethel's mental health. As it was, even without such knowledge, an increasing number who phoned by the end of a conversation with Ethel were usually left in a state of shock and confusion wondering whether they had phoned a law firm or, in error, the local psychiatric hospital and had their phone call answered by some seriously sick patient restrained by a straightjacket connected to a phone to permit occasional restrained communication with the outside world. Geoffrey Brewer favoured the latter theory.

'Hello, Braithwaite Marshall & Co. Can I help you?' Ethel pleasantly enquired.

'Geoffrey Brewer of 15 Sycamore Grove here. I would like to see Mr Braithwaite please.'

'Do you just want to look at him or would you like to talk to him?' Ethel asked.

'No, I mean I would like an appointment to discuss a personal matter.'

'Mr Braithwaite is a lawyer, not a rector, rabbi, priest or social worker. You know he doesn't have time to talk to people about personal matters,' Ethel asserted.

'This is a legal matter I want to discuss with him,' shouted the hapless Geoffrey Brewer. 'I want to talk to him about it and get his advice.'

'You can't talk to him without an appointment. What type of legal matter is it? It doesn't relate to Mr Marshall does it?'

'Well if you like, I'll see... I mean make an appointment instead with Mr Marshall', responded the despairing voice at the end of the phone totally ignorant of the fraught background to the firm's beginnings.

'You can't. He's bloody dead,' Ethel shouted in response.

'I'm very sorry... I, er, didn't know. Well, I would be happy to meet Mr Braithwaite,' said Geoffrey, now doubting whether he really wanted to meet anyone who worked with or had the bad judgement to employ the crazy telephonist who had answered his call.

'You won't discuss Mr Marshall's death with him if I give you an appointment, will you?'

'Oh, of course not. Is he still distressed by it?' Geoffrey Brewer innocently asked, thinking normality had now settled over the conversation. The illusion was quickly dispelled.

'Oh, so you want to meet him to discover whether he is still upset. It wasn't Mr Braithwaite's fault that Michael Marshall died copulating on top of his bloody desk with his secretary,' Ethel shouted in reply.

The click on the line and the subsequent silence confirmed to Ethel that Geoffrey Brewer was just another pervert anxious to talk about Michael Marshall's demise who qualified as an Oxton entrant for the FILS records even without first having a consultation with Cyril. Ethel's only regret was the absence of an opportunity during the phone conversation with the prurient and obviously sick caller to refer him to Moore Bull & Co as she knew that discussions about Michael Marshall's unseemly departure from their firm remained the cause of much angst to both of his former partners.

Unknown to either Moore or Bull, their separate appearances at the local hospital for an angiogram within ten days of what they euphemistically referenced as the firm's 'unhappy event' had resulted in local gossips speculating on what exactly was going on behind the ancient and hallowed doors of Oxton's oldest and most prestigious law firm. Over a year later the daily doings of Moore Bull & Co were still a topic of stimulating and animated discussion in the Ancient Wig, the public house adjacent to the local county court building most frequented by the legal fraternity.

7

CYRIL BRAITHWAITE sat in the Ancient Wig and studied the froth on the top of his pint of beer. It was only shortly after twelve noon and he normally didn't drink pints that time of day. He had finished in court earlier than expected that morning. He couldn't face returning to his office prior to lunch with the threat hanging over him of another three course hamisha, cholesterol-filled meal, lovingly cooked by a doting Ethel Edelwitz.

It had been a good morning for Braithwaite Marshal & Co. His client had been awarded £20,000 and costs for assault against the distraught unisex hairstylist whose embarrassment at misinterpreting Eldon Pettigrew's intentions had been obvious to even the rather thick-skinned His Honour Judge Matthew Gross of Civil Court 6.

Sitting in the hairstylist's cutting chair, a gown draped down to his ankles, Eldon had suddenly been struck on the back of his head with a wooden brush handle by the voluptuous proprietor, Desiree Honeycombe. Desiree's practice of wearing low lying dresses when cutting gent's hair, while intended to arouse the attention of the male clientele sufficiently to attract extra custom, was not intended to affect unduly the probity of what she was anxious to maintain as an expanding and socially respectable business. (Most of her male customers, if asked, would have confessed to experiencing considerable personal expansion whenever Desiree leant over to brush into shape whatever hair they possessed prior to embarking on the cutting process. Fortunately, they were never asked.)

The sight of Eldon's hand rhythmically moving under the gown draped over him to protect his clothes from cut hair had led Desiree to the premature and sadly inaccurate conclusion that Eldon was engaged in the practical application of Cyril's theory of self-help and was bent on bringing his own personal expansion to its logical and physically most satisfying conclusion. The disastrous error had become apparent when her dazed client slumped forward in his chair and the pair of glasses he had been cleaning with his handkerchief under his gown dropped to the floor. Cyril had persuaded the judge that the sum of £2,000 damages proffered by the apologetic and distraught hair stylist was insufficient and that the long-term psychological damage suffered by his client merited a much higher award. A long-haired Eldon Pettigrew had confirmed to the court that since the unprovoked assault he had developed a psychological block to entering barber shops, both single and unisex, and suffered a headache whenever haircuts were mentioned. To prove the point Cyril arranged that halfway through his evidence Eldon became distressed, asked for a glass of water and drank down two aspirin handed to him by Cyril that he just happened to have in his jacket pocket. The ploy had worked a dream. Some of Desiree's replies to Cyril's astute cross-examination had also positively contributed to Cyril's victory and good cheer. He took a few minutes to reflect on his performance and awarded himself five stars.

* * *

Desiree Honeycombe sat demurely in the witness box wearing a modest black dress, her flowing long black hair tied up in a bun. Having briefly and tearfully apologised to Eldon, for 'too forcefully brushing his hair' and describing what occurred as 'an accident', she was informed by Judge Gross, her direct evidence concluded, that she must next answer Mr Braithwaite's questions.

'Miss Honeycombe, your business is called "The Kindest Cut", is that right?' asked Cyril.

'Yes, that's right, Mr Braithwaite,' replied Desiree.

'And for how many years have you been running your business as a unisex hairstylist in Oxton Town?'

'For about ten years,' Desiree replied.

'And throughout those years have both men and women been customers?'

'Yes, they have.'

'And you are used to cutting men's hair.'

'I style hair, Mr Braithwaite, I am not a mere cutter. I am a hair stylist,' Desiree responded somewhat aggrieved.

'Ah yes, so how does that work?' asked Cyril.

'I carefully examine a customer's head of hair, enquire whether he wishes to retain its existing style, which is sometimes no style at all and, if asked, I style or restyle it.'

'That involves, does it not, cutting it?' continued Cyril. 'Essentially, you cut hair. For male customers you are basically their barber, is that not correct?'

'I am a stylist, not a barber,' Desiree emphatically stated. 'Most barbers are just glorified cutters. A style is maintained or created by a mixture of cutting, shaving and brushing. Years of training

44

positively contribute to the stylist's skill. You have to picture the look you are creating in the context of the head of hair presented. Styling also often involves hair colouring but not in the case of Mr Pettigrew.'

'And how long and thick had Mr Pettigrew's hair grown on the day in question?'

'Do I really need to know about the length and thickness of Mr Pettigrew's hair before it was cut, Mr Braithwaite?' intervened a somewhat impatient Judge Gross.

'It's just background, Judge,' explained Cyril. 'The thicker the hair, the less painful the blow. The thinner the hair, the more painful the blow.'

'I don't blow men. I operate a respectable business,' asserted Desiree, clearly confused, before Cyril could ask another question.

Cyril hesitated to let the dust settle, observing a puzzled expression on the judge's face.

'Miss Honeycombe, you do also wash hair, do you not?' Judge Gross intervened in an attempt to restore some sort of order. 'I assume you do not leave it wet? You, like other hair stylists or barbers, blow dry do you not? Is there some problem about blow drying?'

'No, Judge, sorry. I misunderstood the reference.'

Cyril was amused at how a simple word like blow could be so easily misunderstood.

'So, your work does include blow jobs, in the sense of blow drying hair, is that right, Miss Honeycombe?'

'Yes, Mr Braithwaite,' responded the hairstylist, clearly relieved by the clarification.

'But on the day in question, you did not blow dry Mr

Pettigrew's hair, as he arrived having already washed and dried it himself, is that right?'

'Yes, that's right,' replied Desiree.

'Again, I am asking do I really need to know whether Mr Pettigrew's hair was wet or dry, blown or not blown. Isn't this whole thing getting somewhat overblown, Mr Braithwaite?' asserted the judge, looking pleased with his little pun. 'Please move on, Mr Braithwaite, before our time is blown away.'

'Yes, Judge, apologies. Now Miss Honeycombe, moving on from your blowing experience, can I ask again, does Mr Pettigrew have thick or thin hair?'

'It's quite thin,' she replied, glancing over at Eldon.

'So, it afforded little protection to cushion the blow, isn't that right?' asked Cyril, immediately recognising different phraseology might have been more helpful...

'Please Mr Braithwaite could we get away from blows?' directed Judge Gross.

'Yes, sorry Judge,' responded Cyril, swiftly moving on. 'Prior to the day of the unfortunate incident had Mr Pettigrew previously been a customer?'

'Yes, on and off... over about two years.'

'And to be clear, on each occasion he just sought a haircut, nothing more complicated?'

'Yes, that's right.'

'And did he always behave with decorum?'

'I know nothing about his dick or rum, I don't serve alcohol in my shop, just tea or coffee. I do nothing disgusting, Mr Braithwaite. Mine is a respectable business.'

Cyril felt as if he was drowning in the developing confusion.

'I really must intervene again to sort out any misunderstanding,' said Judge Gross. 'Decorum, Miss Honeycombe, was the word used by Mr Braithwaite. He asked whether Mr Pettigrew on previous visits to your establishment always behaved with decorum, that is did he always behave properly. His question has nothing to do with tea or coffee or, indeed, any alcoholic beverage or anatomical part.'

'Oh, sorry, yes he always behaved properly, like any other customer.'

'So, your other customers also behave properly, is that so?' asked Cyril.

'Yes,' she replied anxious to maintain existing good customer relations.

'There aren't others you have had to hit with a brush or any other implement?'

'No, Mr Braithwaite and I don't like the implication. I am a hairstylist not a dominatrix. S and M is not my thing.'

'No one is suggesting it is,' interrupted Judge Gross staring oddly at the witness with an unusual glint in both eyes.

'Now after Mr Pettigrew sat down you draped a large gown over him?' asked Cyril.

'Yes, to protect his clothes from hair that has been cut.'

'You gave him a newspaper to read.'

'Yes, that's right'.

'You would have done that on previous visits?'

'Suppose so, yes.'

'Did you previously notice he wears reading glasses, Miss Honeycombe?'

'Can't say,' came the terse reply.

'Can't say or won't say?' asked Cyril.

'Don't remember. I wouldn't have been thinking about that?'

'So what were you thinking about when you viciously struck my client with the back of a large hairbrush, Miss Honeycombe?'

'I'm not sure. It was an accident.'

'Do you habitually hit your customers accidentally with the back of brushes?' asked Cyril.

'No, of course not. I thought... er suspected there was something going on under his gown,' Desiree explained.

'And what was it that you suspected?' pressed Cyril.

'I'd rather not say, if I don't have to, Judge', she said, looking pleadingly at Judge Gross.

'Well that's up to Mr Braithwaite,' the judge helpfully replied.

'If Judge Gross visited your establishment for a haircut would he be at risk of a spontaneous blow to the head?' asked Cyril.

'Of course not.'

'Well why did you strike Eldon, please explain.'

'I thought he was engaged in some sort of intimacy under the gown.'

'Was there someone else under the gown or sitting on his lap?' enquired Cyril.

'No, of course not.'

'Well what did you see?'

'I saw his hands moving.'

'Are your customers not allowed to move their hands once covered by a gown?' asked Cyril.

'Of course, they are. It was just the way his hands were moving, made me suspicious.'

'Suspicious of what?'

'I'd rather not say.'

'It's ok, Mr Braithwaite, I get the picture,' said Judge Gross again intervening. Turning to the witness he asked, 'What happened after you struck Mr Pettigrew with a brush?'

'He yelled, slumped forward and a pair of glasses fell on the floor.'

'He was cleaning his glasses under the gown, is that not right?' asked Cyril.

'That's right,' she quietly replied.

'Before you viciously assaulted my client did you ask him what he was doing under the gown?'

'No, it just all happened so quickly. I'm truly sorry.'

'You call your business "The Kindest Cut". When hitting Mr Pettigrew with a brush, was that an example of you being cruel to be kind?' asked Cyril.

'You don't need to reply to that, Ms Honeycombe,' intervened Judge Gross. 'I think I've heard enough, Mr Braithwaite, to reach a conclusion. Thank you very much, Miss Honeycombe, you may step down,' he said, ending Cyril's cross-examination, clearly anxious to conclude the hearing and move on to other more pressing legal business.

* * *

Cyril, having been embraced outside the court by his grateful client, then watched him speedily walk up the street to seek a haircut in the nearest barber shop. The award of £20,000 had freed Eldon Pettigrew from his psychological incapacity to have his dome snipped but he was not totally freed from long lasting psychological damage. He would never again set foot inside any business managed by a unisex hairstylist nor let any woman cut his hair.

Cyril's elated reaction to his decisive victory lasted about twenty minutes. It then passed and was rapidly replaced by midday depression. Cyril, as he often did in the Ancient Wig when he had nothing better to do, sat contemplating his life-engaging predicament and ordered another pint. His thoughts were not confined to speculating on the reason for his lack of clients but also extended to the oddities of his relationship with Miranda.

Miranda was spending more time in her mother's house these days than in Larkspur Grove. Since Michael Marshall's death his wife and mother-in-law had developed a mutual addiction to television soaps, series and reality shows which now dominated their days. When Miranda and Martha weren't together watching a television screen they were on their phones speculating about future developments.

Miranda's daily visits to her mother meant they could share 'the televisual experience' together, as Miranda had explained to Cyril after a visit to her therapist. (Cyril understood that characters in most soaps and reality shows always visit their therapist, not their psychiatrist and Cyril at this stage was resigned to Miranda's Americanisms.) Miranda dropped Aloysius off to primary school each morning, then drove straight to her mother's house, only interrupting her daily viewing to do the occasional supermarket shop and to collect Aloysius in the early afternoon. Most time she returned to Martha's after the school collection and having worked through a televisual daytime diet of serial arrived home to put Aloysius to bed by 7.30 p.m. Settling into their lounge room couch she then proceeded to watch recordings of Coronation Street, Eastenders, Greys Anatomy, Made in Chelsea, Game of Thrones, Law and Order, SWAT and repeat episodes of Friends, Sex in the City and Californication.

Cooking most times for both Miranda and Cyril involved zapping pre-packed and flavoured frozen food in the microwave for between two to three minutes whenever either of them or Aloysius were in need of sustenance. Aloysius, almost five years old, still had a daily diet of breast milk which Cyril viewed as just another pre-packed meal, one that Miranda need not unpack and zap in the microwave. Any conversation between Cyril and Miranda was largely confined to the latest soap and reality show happenings watched that day. Miranda had become so confused between soap and reality that her moods and activities were largely dictated by the level of happiness or misery portrayed.

When babies were born, she posted baby cards to the television mother and advice about breast feeding. When weddings took place, a wedding present with alacrity was dispatched to the happy couple. When deaths occurred wreaths were delivered, except when the deceased was Jewish, in which case Miranda had discovered from Ethel Edelwitz the thing to do was to donate £50 to the Jewish National Fund to have trees planted in the deceased's name in Israel or to Magen David Adom for the benefit of Israel's independent emergency response and ambulance service.

Cyril believed that the only normal part of their relationship was the sexual and even this couldn't truly be described as normal. As so many of the soap and reality characters daily portrayed were jumping in and out of bed on a regular basis with whoever took their fancy and never appeared to suffer headaches, need time to wash their hair, to do the ironing or to be inhibited by menstrual pains, Miranda provided Cyril with a selection of bedtime sexual adventures that would have astonished even some of his most athletically committed clients. Cyril's initial ethical reservations about active participation in some of her more outrageous and physically demanding contortions quickly evaporated after a few months consulting with clients about their extramarital activities in the offices of Braithwaite Marshal & Co.

Cyril realised that in the area of sexual intimacy and endeavour Miranda qualified as both wife and mistress. She was quite simply two parts of his sexual ménage-a-trois. Whether his one part could hang in there and keep up the pace was in serious doubt. It eventually dawned on Cyril that Miranda's approach to life and love was a genetic paternal inheritance that probably posed as great a threat to his physical wellbeing as the culinary delights served up by Ethel Edelwitz. He determined that he would ensure his life ran its full natural course and that when his time was finally up and the lottery of life had turned full circle no coroner would describe his cause of death as either cholesterol or sexual. To survive he knew he had to escape from both Miranda and Ethel. However, before he could do so he had to discover a way to make and save some real money.

8

MIRANDA MARSHALL had been a precocious child. From an early age she appeared to take particular delight in doing the exact opposite of what her parents or any other adult in authority, such as a teacher, asked her to do. Her primary school teacher told Martha that for a child of just under five years of age she had an unusually negative attitude. This did not mean she did no school work. It just meant that she would never do the work her teacher asked her to do. If asked to recite some part of the alphabet she would instead count numbers. If told to write down numbers she would instead recite parts of the alphabet. If given a designated seat for school lunch, she would insist on sitting elsewhere. In short, she was contrary.

To Martha and Michael Marshall, the teachers' comments were no surprise. They found Miranda the most difficult and obstinate of all their little Ms.

Michael Marshall when referring to his children, never said 'my children' nor used their individual names, unless doing so was absolutely necessary. He and Martha were 'the big Ms' he used to say less than half jokingly and more than half seriously, and the rest of their family were 'the little Ms'. This appellation also included within it the family dog, Mormon, so named after two clean cut besuited Americans who, coincidentally, called to the Marshall's family home intent on doing God's work the very day the outsized mongrel, as a playful pup, had been left with the Marshalls by a friendly neighbour to test his compatibility with the little Ms. In getting on with the little Ms, he had playfully bitten one of the big over friendly visiting American Ms who had helpfully but rather ineptly tried to retrieve one of the little Ms tennis balls from the mongrel's mouth. As the two Americans speedily departed to the casualty department in Oxton Hospital so that an anti-tetanus injection could be swiftly administered, Michael Marshall pronounced that it was God's wish that they keep the dog and named him Mormon. It was the first and only religious pronouncement of his entire life.

Mormon as he grew older, proved to be as unpredictable, unmanageable and as contrary as Miranda. Recognising each other as kindred spirits, they stuck closely together.

At ten years of age Miranda and Mormon regularly went off together for a walk in the nearby local park with Martha's usual instruction ringing in their ears.

'Don't go walking in the woods. Just stay around the playground, dog run and football pitches.' They would immediately then go walk through the woods.

'Never talk to strangers,' Martha ordered. Most days when she went to the park Miranda deliberately looked out for strangers to engage.

'Who are you?' Miranda would impishly stop and ask whoever happened to be sitting alone on a park bench. She then struck up animated conversations that could last for up to twenty minutes. Fortunately for Miranda, the loyal presence of Mormon, unknown to her or her canine guardian, saved her from attack on six separate occasions by some of Oxton's better known police-registered paedophiles. Each of them had already been involuntary guests of Her Majesty's Prison Service. Confronted by a red haired, green eyed, freckled, precocious ten-year-old accompanied by a mongrel that looked like a cross between an Alsatian, a Rottweiler and tyrannous rex, all six of the dangerous seriously dysfunctional had independently decided for reasons of self-preservation to ignore what they wrongly perceived as Miranda's provocative presence and instead concentrate on the natural beauty of the park's flora and fauna.

As Miranda approached her mid-teens, Martha, conscious of her growing physical attributes and rebellious nature, counselled her about matters sexual and, in particular, the need to avoid both pregnancy and sexually transmitted infection. On matters sexual, unknown to Martha, she already enjoyed a full doctoral education deserving the awarding of a PhD in sexology as a result of her regularly quietly observing other, but older, little Ms nocturnal exploits on the rather battered basement playroom couch through a hole in the door of the playroom toy cupboard.

On nights when she knew Melvin, Maurice, Melissa or Marigold were out on a date, Miranda would silently creep downstairs after her parents had gone to bed and hide in the toy cupboard awaiting the arrival of a brother or sister together with that evening's companion. Often she would fall asleep, only to be awoken by creaking springs, gasps for breath and ghostly moans of writhing spirits cavorting passionately on the couch which was only an arm's reach away from the discrete viewing peephole made by her in the cupboard door. During each late-night performance she dare not move, sneeze nor cough for fear of discovery and had to remain both still and quiet. Even giggling was strictly forbidden.

On occasions, she struggled to contain herself when confronted by Melvin's desperate struggles to put on a condom. Six years her senior, when he arrived home with a date, he seemed to spend more time wrestling with rubber than seducing his guest.

The cupboard adventures finally came to a tragic end one fateful Wednesday night when Miranda was almost seventeen. Mormon unexpectedly bounded through the playroom door, which had been negligently left open. Having caught Melvin with his top off, trousers down and his latest conquest lying totally naked on the couch, the irascible dog briefly assaulted Melvin's bottom with a quick lick. He then chose to ignore the playroom naturalists and yapped and whimpered happily at the cupboard door. Upon the door being rapidly opened by Melvin, Miranda's uninvited presence was instantly revealed.

Miranda's career as the family voyeur came to an abrupt and painful end. After the verbal lashing and smack on her bottom she received from Melvin as she fled out of the basement she never again dared to sit it out in the toy cupboard. Unknown to Miranda, from that night on whenever a boyfriend or girlfriend visited the Marshalls' playroom the toy cupboard was always first inspected before the start of any real action.

No longer able to watch, Miranda determined after her seventeenth birthday that her time to experiment had arrived. For the next six years she worked her way through a series of boyfriends, all of whom had one thing in common, none of them possessed a first, second or third name nor a surname that started with the thirteenth letter of the alphabet. She had developed what was at that time the unknown but later discovered and now widely recognised psychiatric condition of an M phobia. Her mind and body, in rebellion against all parental upbringing and conditioning, compelled her to make an amorous play for as many non-Ms as possible. She slowly and deliberately worked her way through her early alphabet phase, followed by her middle alphabet phase and her late alphabet phase ending with the letter Z. By the time she hit twenty-one, she had managed by a combination of first names and surnames to have sexually experimented with all twenty-five letters of the alphabet that appealed to her. She had even managed to overcome the difficulties posed by the twenty first, twenty second, twenty-fourth and twenty-sixth letters. This could be confirmed by Urel Uzellski, Vincent Velurri, Harold Xeng and Jonathan Zeus.

Cyril did not know that Miranda's voyeuristic activity and empirical experimentation had resulted in her sexual education reaching post-doctoral university status by the time they first met. Also unknown to Cyril was that his literally coming on the scene coincided with Miranda having almost completed a unique reverse journey travelling sexually through the entire alphabet from Z to A. Her bonking a CB, as in Cyril Braithwaite, and then giving birth to an A, as in Aloysius, completed a preordained circle and made absolute sense to those, and there were few, who understood the debilitating impact of alphabet phobias and fetishes. Unknown to Miranda or even Cyril, her marriage to Cyril and insistence that their son be named Aloysius was just an external manifestation of an invisible condition of which the scientific, medical and mental health community were largely ignorant. It was also unknown that five years after Michael Marshall's death an 'M' would enter Miranda's life, she would conquer her 'M' phobia, acquire Michael Marshall's 'M' fetish and both her and Cyril's world would change for ever.

9

ETHEL EDELWITZ WAS convinced that Cyril was secretly in love with her. She also believed that the psychological repercussions of Michael Marshall's death had resulted in Cyril lacking the mental capacity to fully recognise his feelings for fear of unwittingly revealing them to another in an unguarded moment of drunken frankness in the Ancient Wig. Cyril's love for her, Ethel reasoned, was a part of his secret subconscious world which would inevitably emerge from his innermost being into the light of day. Her mission was to plan for their inevitable future life together after Cyril's anticipated day of personal revelation.

Ethel's mother had imbued her daughter with two life-engaging ambitions. First, she had to marry a millionaire. Second, he had to be circumcised. The fact that her mother also intended that he be Jewish was initially lost on Ethel, who for some inexplicable reason did not grasp the fact that her mother believed Judaism and circumcision to be synonymous. The fact that you would usually have one with the other resulted in her mother, who had no personal experience in the matter, not realising you can have the other without the one! Cyril, Ethel knew, was no millionaire. Whether he was circumcised or not was to her still something of a mystery.

Ethel was determined to dramatically improve Cyril's finances and also to discover whether physiologically he was correctly sculptured. Happily, unknown to Cyril, as if he had known it would have had a profound effect on his personal serenity, Ethel was also determined that if Cyril's manhood did not live up to her mother's expectations she would have it redesigned. Just as she was devoted to Cyril, Ethel was devoted to fulfilling her mother's limited lifetime ambitions. She was determined that she would ultimately shack up with a very rich and very circumcised Cyril Braithwaite even if she had to circumcise Cyril herself. Whether she would be able to persuade him after their destined marriage to change his name to her own preferred choice of Braithwitz was only a minor source of uncertainty. A few more plates of chopped liver and a few more knaidlach filled bowls of chicken soup she reasoned on the basis of Darwin's theory of evolution would inevitably result in Cyril himself dumping the 'waite' for a 'witz'. By now, she believed, he was at least halfway there.

Cyril in his innocence had no inkling that at this stage in their non-relationship Ethel believed him to be a half witz. Whether making him a full witz would turn him into the Yiddisha boy Ethel's mother had always yearned for as a son-in-law was not to the forefront of Cyril's concerns. Such a name change in Ethel's simple reasoning would ensure the five children she hoped to have with Cyril would each be a little Braithwitz. Although she had always hated the first part of her surname and disliked the last part of Cyril's, she believed the first part of his joined to the last part of hers to be really classy. Why should she not bring some class into their lives, she frequently asked when engaged in silent but satisfying conversation with herself? Unfortunately for Cyril no one, other than Ethel, ever replied to the silent question posed. Probably because the response of anyone else was never sought.

10

BARTHOLOMEW BULL knew something must be wrong. In twenty-five years of legal practice, until the start of that very week, he had never heard a story like it. Now it seemed within the space of five days Oxton was experiencing an epidemic.

Jocelyn Brewer sobbed gently into her petite white handkerchief as Bartholomew stared at the card she had handed to him. It read:

> Your husband is fucking Sheila Endwhistle.
> Be on your guard.
> From a friend.

The card was white front and back. Each word on the card was composed of letters or words clearly cut out of a newspaper and pieced together to produce a sentence. Obviously the 'friend' had more difficulty with some words compared to others. For example, the word 'husband' was obviously a single word cut out and glued to the card, whilst 'fucking' was composed of individual letters of the alphabet painstakingly extracted and then stuck together. It did not take a genius or even a solicitor to conclude that whatever paper had been cut up, didn't usually go to print with such unpleasant crudities. 'Endwhistle' had given the anonymous author less difficulty containing the two popular and much-used words 'End' and 'whistle'. The simple expedient of writing over it with a black marker pen had transformed the 'e' in end into a capital.

'I don't know who Sheila Endwhistle is or when Geoffrey started doing that awful thing to her,' wailed Jocelyn Brewer, responding to Bartholomew's gentle questioning. 'The card just arrived in the post this morning after Geoffrey went to work and I rang your secretary for an urgent appointment,'

'Well prior to the card's arrival had you been having any marital problems?' he asked.

'No, none at all,' sobbed Jocelyn. 'We've been married eight years and we've never had a single upset. Geoffrey's an accountant and he works too hard and I'm always telling him to try to get home earlier at night because I worry about him but other than that everything is fine with us and our two kids are fine and I love my part-time job as Dr Norman Zendlove's receptionist and I enjoy housework and cooking and we get on very well and he brings home flowers every Friday night and all our in-laws get on and he has never shown any interest in other women...'

'Don't upset yourself further, I understand, it's alright,' said Bartholomew, using the distraught woman's first pause for breath to interrupt the verbal locomotive she was driving through his brain with her high-pitched, grief-stricken, never-ending, punctuation-lacking reply.

Bartholomew didn't really understand at all but he couldn't admit that to a fee-paying client. Like all solicitors, he had long since realised the importance of pretending to understand everything a client told him, even if he didn't, and of pretending to have the legal answer to a problem, even if he hadn't. He understood the importance of his clients having confidence in his ability to give advice and provide legal representation and also, where possible, feeling positive when departing from his office, even if they shouldn't. Without that feeling of confidence and positivity he knew that it was unlikely that his consultation fee would be paid. Sometimes, even with it, it was difficult to get paid as most clients believed their solicitors charged too much. Even though they regularly protested that they didn't, few clients believed that.

All of this had flashed through Bartholomew's mind during the momentary pause for breath taken by his distraught client. It had also flashed through his mind that because of the duty of solicitor and client confidentiality, he couldn't tell Jocelyn Brewer that over the previous four days he had seen seven similar messages sent by the same or an unspecified number of other anonymous 'friends' to seven other similarly emotionally stressed out clients.

'You don't have enough evidence here to obtain a divorce,' he advised, like most good lawyers focusing on the facts. It didn't occur to him to ask whether his client actually wanted a divorce or whether she just wanted to stop Geoffrey doing 'the awful thing' to Sheila Endwhistle so delicately described in that morning's unsolicited postal bombshell so that they could get on with their lives without the unknown Endwhistle coming between them. (The rather poorly phrased last half of this sentence should not be taken to mean that Sheila ever had or would literally or sexually speaking come between Jocelyn and Geoffrey whatever other damage she might unknowingly do to their relationship. While Sheila did not mind her climactic moments being viewed as a spectator sport there was no chance Jocelyn would want to

62

spectate on Sheila having such a moment with Geoffrey, nor participate in a ménage-a-trois.)

'Of course,' continued Bartholomew Bull, 'the card might be malicious and the allegation that your husband is having an extramarital affair may be untrue.'

'But why would anyone post me that card inside a typed addressed envelope if it is untrue, and why use newsprint when the address on the envelope is typed?' asked Jocelyn looking puzzled.

'I really don't know, but before you do anything you could get a private detective to investigate. If it is true and you decide on a divorce, you will need to verify the allegation. You should do that first before you say anything to Geoffrey so that he doesn't attempt to cover his tracks. If it's not true, you won't have to say anything at all to him about this and you can avoid causing unnecessary upset, but we may discover the identity of the card's author, why it was sent and who Sheila Endwhistle is.'

Fifteen minutes later Jocelyn Brewer having departed with the private investigator's business card furnished by Bartholomew in her handbag, the bemused lawyer sat behind his desk and stared quizzically at the eight different cards laid out on it. They all contained newspaper cut out warnings to Oxton residents that their spouses were engaged in various luridly described acts of marital infidelity. Never one to jump to overhasty conclusions, Bartholomew thought it all too much to be a coincidence. Whether someone in Oxton Town had on their own initiative appointed themselves as Oxton's marital policeman or policewoman to warn the unsuspecting of their spouses' infidelity or the cards were the literary ravings of a local candidate for the

Monster Raving Looney Party he did not know. Either way the cards were a guaranteed fee-earner and he was on to fifteen percent of the fees that his eight clients would pay to his recommended private detective. Another good thing was that not a single one of the Oxton Eight had either directly or indirectly asked a single question or made any comment about Michael Marshall's death. Until then most of his new clients couldn't resist the temptation. Undoubtedly, he would have been less relaxed about it all, if he had known at that very moment his own wife was sitting crying in Cyril Braithwaite's office having become another unhappy recipient of an unexpected anonymous postal communication at 11 a.m. that very morning.

11

FOR TWO REASONS Ethel phoned Cyril to the Ancient Wig at lunch time, interrupting his rebellious consumption of the pub's specialty – a smoked ham and salad sandwich with the pub's 'world famous' homemade sweet chutney and pickles. The first was to complain that he had not warned her that he might not return to the office by one o'clock and that as a result his lunch was overcooked and inedible. The second was to inform him that an emergency had arisen and that he should return as soon as possible as a clearly distressed Pamela Bull was sitting in the waiting room demanding an instant consultation. She threw in a comment that she thought she could revive the tzimmes if he was still hungry but that his spiced lamb chops were beyond redemption.

Ignoring Ethel's revival plan and determined to eat strictly non-kosher, Cyril returned to his table, slowly finished his sandwich and lowered what remained of his pint of Oxton's best ale. Thirty minutes later he drove back to his office.

> Bartholomew screws the Redhead.
> Be warned by Marshall's fate.
> From a friend.

Sitting alongside his office coffee table with Pamela Bull, Cyril studied the white card with the newsprint stuck on message and asked all the right questions. No, she had not suspected her husband of screwing the redhead or anyone else; yes, they were getting on fine; yes, she had once had a little fling with the gardener six years ago but it only lasted for that summer's grass cutting season; no, Bart knew nothing about it; the gardener was now planting his seed on another patch, namely Christee Jenkinson's patch, three doors up; she had not discussed the contents of the card with Bart; she did not know the identity of the friendly correspondent; she supposed the redhead to be Bart's secretary, Cindy Bretson, and she perceived Cyril to be something of an expert on the subject with, perhaps, some inside knowledge.

Explaining that he had neither inside nor outside knowledge of Bartholomew's alleged affair, Cyril asked some more pertinent questions.

'Other than the content of the card do you have any reason to believe that Bart... er, Bartholomew has anything more than a working relationship with Miss Bretson?' he enquired, immediately regretting his choice of words in light of the well-known working relationship of the late lamented Michael Marshall with his equally lamented secretary in the very same office.

'I've no other reason to suspect anything is going on,' Pamela unhappily replied. Happily for Cyril she did not refer to the type of working relationship that Cyril was starting to suspect to be more usual than exceptional in his deceased father-in-law's former law firm.

'Except for one thing that occurred after Michael Marshall's rather... er unusual death,' Pamela continued. 'Bart was very anxious to have his heart checked. It seemed a sensible precaution then but I am now wondering was there more to it than I realised? I mean, Bart doesn't have weight problems and was some ten years younger than Michael at the time. He also keeps himself fit. Why would he have gone for an angiogram unless something was up?'

Cyril successfully resisted the temptation to ask her to identify the 'something' which might be up and maintained a seriously concerned expression.

'Oh, I don't think that the angiogram proves anything. It's all the rage nowadays to get one of those executive check-ups. After Michael Marshall's unexpected death it was quite natural that other members of the firm would have themselves checked. I don't think having an angiogram means you are seducing or being seduced by your secretary,' Cyril reasonably replied. He carefully avoided any reference to any gossip about Moore Bull & Co circulating in the Ancient Wig. In the context of the firm's history a partner having an angiogram might be regarded as a public declaration of infidelity to some beer imbibing members of the legal fraternity but Cyril knew it would be of no value as evidence in any divorce case.

Ten minutes later Cyril and Pamela parted company. It was agreed that Cyril would do nothing at all until he again heard from Pamela. Doing nothing at all was one of the things in life that Cyril found most appealing.

12

JOSHUA SHOSHOWSKI had never experienced a week like it. It was just eighteen months since he had rented a room on the fourth floor of the semi-derelict building on Deaver Street and business had been very slow. The letter set nameplate on the door into his room was already the worse for wear reading

Jos ua Sho o ski,
Pr ate Detective

Having taken to heart Cyril's theory of self-help, Joshua had financed his first month's rent with the cash he had received from trading in the car radio and music system he had in a moment of spontaneity stolen from a car parked near the courthouse, not knowing it was Cyril's. Thereafter, he vowed to himself it would be his last act of criminality. If he was going to set himself up in business, he knew he would need some start-up capital. His final and most successful criminal act of vehicular grand larceny Joshua regarded simply as the general public's investment in his future of non-crime.

'If you are going to start up on your own,' the pamphlet given to him by his designated work coach in the Department for Work and Pensions Job Centre Office advised, 'work in an area with which you are familiar.' As he had been investigated more times than most, Joshua decided working as a private detective fitted the bill. The circular letter, followed by a reminder email, sent by him to all of Oxton Towns solicitor's firms seeking work (except for Cyril's, who he wanted one day to surprise with his success) had, until that week, been of only limited help in obtaining work. He had made just enough money to survive and keep the rent up to date by tracing the whereabouts of four lost cats, three lost dogs, an elderly retired chiropodist suffering from dementia who wandered off from his care home and a 1935 Rolls Royce stolen from the private garden of a local car collector. His greatest triumph to date was his rescuing from incarceration by her father in her family home a Nisheen Munktakyada, the Pakistani mistress of a television salesman, whose family disapproved of her broadcast connection. The salesman had paid him handsomely for delivering a clearly ecstatic Nisheen to his home where to this day they still happily resided.

Initially forgetting to tell the job centre officer that he was self-employed, receiving unemployment and support allowance had also helped Joshua keep life and limb together and to pay for a small advert published weekly in the Oxton Weekly News. Now, in the space of one week, eight new clients had arrived in his office recommended by the towns oldest and most prestigious solicitors' firm, Moore Bull & Co. His second circular email offering a fifteen percent kickback for referrals had proved spectacularly successful.

'Oh Mr Shooski, I hope you can get to the bottom of it for me, this whole Endwhistle thing is so upsetting,' said Jocelyn Brewer as she paid to Joshua the eighth £2,000 deposit received by him that week for taking on a case.

'I'll do my best, you can rest assured, Mrs Brewer,' Joshua responded reassuringly, unconcerned by the name change caused by the fallen letter set.

'I'll do my best,' he repeated ten minutes later as she exited from his ramshackle office and descended the shaky stairs out into the street.

Eight clients, five wives, three husbands, all the recipients of messages from an anonymous 'friend' warning them that their spouses were variously screwing, bonking, pumping, humping, deflowering, stuffing, gumming and fucking five named women and three named men, all of whose existence and identity had to be confirmed and the truth of the allegations made investigated. Sipping his fourth celebratory Maitai, his favourite cocktail, in Maxwells Restaurant as the waiter prepared Joshua's first ever crepe suzette beside his table, he studied copies of the eight carded messages he had laid out on the table before him. There was no doubt his eight clients had received messages from the same 'friend' who had clearly developed an extended vocabulary to describe acts of human intimacy. While he conducted an investigation into his client's spouses and their alleged peccadillos, he decided he would ask each of his new clients to supply him with a list of their friends to ascertain whether any of them coincided. He could not for confidentiality reasons reveal to any of them the fact that each of them had apparently received a message from the same person claiming to be a 'friend' who, he guessed was unlikely to be a real friend at all!

Confidentiality, Joshua understood was in everyone's interests and, more particularly, in his own interest. If he eventually established the cards to have been sent by a single friendly nut case, there could be some controversy later on if the clients learnt of his charging fees to each of them for revealing to each the identity of the same mentally deranged messenger. Satisfied clients and happy solicitors were Joshua's objective and the avoiding of all possible upset and controversy. Anything different jeopardised positive recommendations, the referral of additional new clients and his undertaking future profitable investigations.

13

CYRIL WAS PUZZLED. Why would anyone anonymously post a card to Pamela Bull warning her of Bartholomew's alleged infidelity? If it was true and the card's author had some genuine concern for Pamela why not simply phone her and arrange to meet? Why go to the trouble of anonymously posting to her a card with a message composed of newspaper cut-outs? It made no sense.

Pamela had agreed that before Cyril took any action she would first check out what, if anything, was going on in Moore Bull & Co and keep a close eye on both Bart and Cindy Bretson. Dropping in regularly without prior warning to Bart's office was her plan. She also intended to make love on a nightly basis at home, knowing that most times Bart was a twice a week man. She reckoned that such increased marital activity would not only reduce his interest in philandering but also reduce his capacity to philander even if he wished to.

'Joachim Joxum, your 4.30 p.m. road traffic accident appointment is here,' announced Ethel over the office intercom, interrupting Cyril's musings.

'Send him in, please,' responded Cyril, happy that his final appointment had nothing to do with failed marriages, anonymous messages or sexual encounters. He opened the new client file sitting on his desk which he had read earlier that day. Inside there were four charge sheets all alleging driving offences, the most serious being 'the dangerous and reckless driving of a motor vehicle endangering life and to the detriment of property and the general public' carrying a penalty of up to five years' imprisonment. Although Cyril had lost interest in general criminal work after the Joshua Shoshowski episode, road traffic charges were a different matter. They usually paid well, most of the alleged offenders were respectable and the court hearings were usually comprehensively reported in the Oxton Weekly News, resulting in good free publicity. A novel plea on behalf of a client always guaranteed front-page coverage and attracted new business outside the marital area.

The high-pitched, pre-pubescent soprano-toned larynx that introduced itself, after Ethel had directed the new client into his office, momentarily startled Cyril and instantly demolished his train of thought. An hour later as he exchanged goodbyes with an obviously seriously discombobulated Joachim Joxum, Cyril determined that this could be his last road traffic case.

'Why is it,' he asked the nine-foot rubber tree growing complacently in a plant pot precariously sitting on a small coffee table in the far corner of his office, 'that I can't get ordinary simple road traffic accidents, perhaps just involving one or two tragic deaths? Why is it that when they come to me complaining of a barber's assault or to be defended for reckless driving there always has to be an extra ingredient? Why is it that their private parts always feature somewhere in the story? What have I done to deserve so many of these clients? Why does all the crazy stuff end up on my desk?'

Cyril spent the next half hour contemplating these and many other similar questions of no particular interest or importance or even of relevance to the rest of this story or to the future life of the unfortunate Joachim Joxum. At 6 p.m. in his usual state of self-induced despondency, he retired disillusioned to the Ancient Wig for his evening pint. It had happened yet again. Despite all his loving care and daily feed of water and expensive nutrients, he had got no response. The rubber tree had come up with no answers to his searching cross-examination of either his role in the legal profession or of the meaning of life. Resigned to his fate, Cyril hoped that his half hour of conversation with the plant would at least positively contribute to the plant's wellbeing and growth as Dr Jacob Horowitz, the publicly acclaimed horticulturist, claimed. Unknown to Cyril, five minutes into the questioning, the plant had not only stopped growing for that day but had fallen fast asleep. It had heard it all before.

14

'SHE SAT UP IN HER bed and stretched demurely. He lay motionless beside her, his jet-black hair stretching down the back of his neck, a relaxed smile of contentment on his face. His broad, muscular, bronzed arms lay on the white soft silk sheets and she hazily recalled the way in which he had carried her up the stairs and effortlessly lain her down on the bed less than two hours earlier. As she ran her fingers through his long, soft, shining black hair he carefully undressed her, starting by slowly unbuttoning her blue cotton blouse and, as he did so, gently nibbled her right ear. She gasped at his touch as he unhooked the front of her bra to reveal her brown pert nipples and cupped her firm white breasts in his two large strong sun-tanned hands. She stretched up to reach his mouth with her tongue as she became increasingly aroused. She then lay back onto the bed feeling his tongue move down between her breasts, passed her belly button, in the direction of her aching wet pussy.

'She reached out to feel his hardness and then swiftly unzipped the front of his dark blue denim jeans to release the pent-up energy within. As his tongue traced invisible shapes on the inside of her right thigh, feline like, he turned his body around so she could remove his jeans as he undid her short skirt and pulled down her wet panties. After he pulled his sports top over his head they lay naked on the bed locked together in a passionate timeless twilight zone, teasing each other, yearning for fulfilment but neither wanting to allow the moment end. Each on the edge of the precipice, both struggling to avoid the fall. Suddenly, without warning, their world seismically erupted and they both fell together, gasping for breath, overwhelmed by their spectacular orgasms and rush of emotion.

'She awoke first. She watched him turn onto his side and studied the muscles running down the back of his sculptured legs. She again lay down, wrapping her body around him, her cold smooth hands slowly brushing over his crotch, her breasts pressed up against his back. She felt him stir and as he turned to meet her, she knew they would again make love.'

The snoring beside Miranda Braithwaite increased in intensity and broke the spell. She put the book that she was reading down on her bedside table and poked Cyril in the ribs, making him turn over. He remained sound asleep. The snoring temporarily stopped. It was 9.30 a.m. on a Sunday morning. She had been sitting up in bed reading for over an hour lost in a literary sexual fantasy. She realised it was time to make a decision. Should she prepare the piece of beef for slow roasting in the oven or wait until later and cook it in the microwave's speed oven? Before reaching any conclusion Cyril's snoring resumed at an increased decibel level and he unknowingly contributed to the decision-making process. Miranda concluded that she should instantly get up, escape from the bedroom, flavour the roast, let it marinate for a while and then cook it in the oven. After the flavouring she could relax and read the book's next chapter over a cup of hot tea and a brown toasted scone in the quiet of the conservatory, well away from Cyril's repetitive bedside sound bites. It wasn't every Sunday Miranda was spared making breakfast for Aloysius, who was overnighting with her mother who had asked for some exclusive granny time. She might as well make the most of it.

If only, Miranda thought as she descended the stairs, book in hand, fiction and fact could coincide. If only that could be her lying between the soft silk sheets snuggled into a bronzed Adonis making passionate love. Unknown to Miranda, as far as Cyril was concerned, he would have been quite happy for her to do so. At least he then might have benefited from a night off!

15

'UNFORTUNATELY, Mr Braithwitz... er... sorry, Mr Braithwaite is not in a position to see you. I would suggest as an alternative Moore Bull & Co.'

'But I would prefer Mr Braithwaite.'

'I'm sorry, that's not possible,' Ethel responded, offering no explanation and rapidly putting down the phone before one could be sought by the bemused caller.

It was the twelfth such call in two weeks. A number of the FILS folders were about to be reopened and this time the circumstances surrounding Michael Marshall's death would not be the main pre-occupation of the caller or the principal topic of conversation during requested consultations.

* * *

Two days before Joachim Joxum's case was to be heard in court, Cyril found himself again having lunch and a pint in the Ancient Wig, this time with Joachim's prosecuting barrister, Reginald Derby KC.

'It's quite simple,' Cyril nonchalantly explained, 'as Mr Joxum drove through the Barton Street and Chapel Road junction with his trousers down and his girlfriend's head deeply buried in his crotch his mobile phone rang. At the very moment he answered it a wasp flew in through the open car window. Still holding the phone in his right hand, he took a swipe at the wasp with his left, missed it and accidentally hit his girlfriend on the back of her head. This resulted in her involuntarily closing her mouth and inadvertently biting off his dick. This unexpected finale to what up to then had been a rather pleasant afternoon's drive caused my client, unsurprisingly, to lose his concentration, veer to the right and drive straight through the Midland Bank's plate glass window. The panic-stricken and seriously gagging girlfriend then tumbled out the front passenger door, stumbled onto the road and threw up the dismembered member under the wheels of a passing truck, rendering its reconstruction, reattachment and healing impossible. Fortunately, no one was hurt, except my client, who the medics report will never again be the man he was. Not only will he be unable to live up to his peculiar nickname of the Lollipop Man but his voice has permanently increased by six octaves and he still walks with a limp.'

'Do you really expect me to believe that story?' Reginald asked.

'Do you really think anyone in their right mind could invent such a ridiculous story?' Cyril replied with exasperation. 'Only an idiot would try to make up such an event to get his client off. Unfortunately for Mr Joxum and also unfortunately for his still traumatised girlfriend, who is available to give evidence, it is all totally true. If the case goes ahead, a not guilty plea will be entered to all the charges against him. We shall be claiming that the entire affair was not due to my client's recklessness but due to an act of God, that is, the wasp's unexpected attempt to hitch a lift at a rather delicate and inappropriate moment. My client is a travelling salesman and will lose his job if his licence is suspended. On the other hand, if you will accept a guilty plea on a careless driving charge and support my application to the court to only impose a small fine, due to the extenuating circumstances, you will be certain to record a conviction and be saved the time and hassle of going to trial.'

'But my going to trial is no great hassle, it's what I do most days,' came the nonchalant reply.

'Ah yes,' Cyril continued, 'but, if we do go to trial, we'll ask for a jury. There must be a strong possibility that out of compassion a jury will deliver a not guilty verdict and let him off. We can even produce his squashed missing private part in evidence, as its mangled remains are currently being preserved by Dr Sharon Scott in Oxton County Hospital's laboratory. Indeed, my client still feels some affection and affinity for it and has taken to visiting it regularly. I have seen it in a photo and take my word, it is not a pretty sight. The acceptance of a guilty plea on the lesser charge would avoid the rather unpleasant headlines the tabloids would inevitably run on the story if a full-blown trial were to take place and save court time to deal with the real villains,' concluded Cyril, concealing his delight in his deliberately deployed choice of phrase reminiscent of court room exchanges during the Desiree Honeycombe case.

Reginald Derby KC silently considered Cyril's proposition.

'Why is it, Cyril, that you get all the totally weird cases?' he asked.

'I don't know. I keep asking myself that. I do seem to attract them,' sighed Cyril. 'Well do we have a deal?'

'You have a deal all right,' replied the KC, surrendering to the inevitable.

To cement the deal Cyril ordered them each another pint. Once it was drunk, he intended to rapidly telephone his client and tell him the good news. He would then return to his office and share it with the rubber tree.

'By the way, Cyril, what happened to the wasp?' Reginald enquired with a smile as he sipped his second pint.

'Just this morning we served it with a subpoena, as we expected it to be a hostile witness,' replied Cyril chuckling.

'Wish I never asked,' commented Reginald. They then silently sat together individually contemplating the vicissitudes of a lawyer's life and finished their ale.

16

G EOFFREY BREWER was seated in the recently opened New York style deli on Oxton's high street lost in thought. It was two days from D Day for income tax returns to be sent to the Inland Revenue. Like all accountancy practices, big and small, right across Britain, he was overrun with calls from panic-stricken self-employed clients conned by the revenue into believing that if they did not get their annual tax returns and their tax payments in on time and the tax paid exactly right, not only would they have to pay a massive sum of interest that could result in their bankruptcy but that it was inevitable they would become unwilling guests in one of his majesty's less salubrious lock-up institutions run by the prison service. The televised warnings to get your returns and payments in on time, emphasising the dire consequences of failing to do so, had clearly unhinged an unexpectedly large number of his usually hardheaded and tight-fisted self-employed clientele.

Geoffrey had lost count of the number of clients who had recently revealed undeclared income they now wished for the first time to declare. The town of Oxton, he concluded, was overrun by income tax cheats and criminals. He reckoned that if the revenue were to ever prosecute and have them all jailed, Oxton would rapidly become a ghost town like some of the abandoned old shanty towns of the Wild West.

As Geoffrey sank his teeth into a smoked salmon and cream cheese bagel with pickles his train of thought was interrupted by a stunning blonde woman wearing a see-through blouse unusually risqué for daytime Oxton Town. Unexpectedly protruding through the blouse were two prominent pert brown nipples.

'Seat spare?' she asked.

'No bra,' he replied, spontaneously articulating the instant optical assessment of the unexpected communicated to his brain which was at that exact moment struggling to cope with the unanticipated delights on public display. A man more usually committed to the cerebral than the physical, Geoffrey fought a losing battle to unscramble the significance of the message his ears were trying to transmit so that he could extend a coherent and welcoming reply. The inexplicable non-sequitur of his response didn't put off his uninvited tormentor, who blissfully unaware of what he said, due to the deafening hub-hub of the surrounding masticating diners, proceeded to sit down on the brash, albeit accurate assumption that she would be a welcome addition to any solo male occupied lunchtime table with a vacant chair. Whether she was oblivious to the uncontrollable stirrings her publicly displayed brown parts had catalysed in a non-cerebral part of her newly acquired lunchtime companion is uncertain.

'Yes, of course, sit down,' Geoffrey belatedly responded to the already seated, his various confused senses once again co-ordinating. Introductions were called for he reasoned.

'I'm Geoffrey, Geoffrey Brewer,' he announced uncertainly.

'Right on,' came the reply in a readily recognisable New York accent as the hand he extended for a hello handshake was unceremoniously slapped down onto the table. 'Hilda's the name.

The question is, Jeff, do you arm wrestle?'

'Well, er... not usually. Not usually at lunchtime anyway?' responded the confused newly named accountant who up to that moment had always resisted the blight of name abbreviation.

'C'mon, don't be a schmuck, what's life all about if you can't have fun?' enthused Hilda.

Before Geoffrey or Jeff, pick your preference, could say any more, his right hand was held in a vicelike grip and, as he struggled frantically to assert the physical superiority of the male species, he silently acknowledged to himself that he was fighting a losing battle. The pain in his right arm was less of a personal physical distraction than the strange spontaneous throbbing between his legs, which was rapidly approaching a dangerously public climactic crescendo. Just as he reckoned the game was up and he was about to lose all control, Hilda loosened her grip, allowing Geoffrey push for victory.

Having snatched victory from the jaws of defeat, Geoffrey realised he had totally lost interest in edibles. To co-ordinate his audibles with his opticals was the main problem. Struggling to dismiss all nipple-centric thoughts, he concluded that some casual conversation would be appropriate. But what to say?

'Do you arm wrestle regularly at lunchtime?' he lamely asked, wanting to say something really memorable but unable to think of anything.

'Only when I see someone I want to hump one day,' Hilda replied, having swallowed the first bite of her reuben and pickle with extra cheese mountain-sized sandwich.

'Oh,' Geoffrey imaginatively responded, his brain befuddled in a brown haze. No one had ever before described Geoffrey, or even the newly named Jeff, as a person they wanted to hump. Not even Jocelyn, his wife, who was the only person with whom he had ever engaged in humping.

It wasn't until shortly after 3 p.m. that Geoffrey walked unsteadily out of the deli struggling to come to terms with his bizarre unconventional lunchtime encounter. A man who had never previously had an adulterous thought, Geoffrey discovered that he had become incapable of any other type of thought. His pace increased as his office building came into view. Geoffrey determined to refocus and tackle the growing mound of tax returns requiring calculation and submission to His Majesty's Revenue. As he sat behind his desk, files neatly arranged, laptop tax programme online and calculator poised for action, he fought determinedly to concentrate on the work in hand. An hour later he surrendered. The only objects Geoffrey truly wished to take in hand were the pert brown nipples that had tormented his lunchtime thoughts. Retiring to the men's room to seek release for his pent-up emotions, he gave satisfying physical expression to a philosophy of life which he did not know had been first pioneered in Oxton by one of the towns best-known recently qualified lawyers. While Cyril Braithwaite without any doubt was Oxton's leading proponent of self-service and self-fulfilment, Geoffrey was about to become a devoted disciple.

* * *

Standing unnoticed on the corner of the high street opposite the deli throughout Geoffrey's lunchtime exploits was a strange, tall, sallow-faced man with black curly hair wearing a blue anorak taking pictures and writing notes. Joshua Shoshowski was for the first time that day coincidentally following Jocelyn Brewer's husband and believed that he had struck pay dirt, or at least dirt of some description. The card received by his client in the post, he reasoned, must be right. Here was his stakeout having an extended lunch with the person he understandably but wrongly concluded must be Sheila Endwhistle. The woman he watched Geoffrey arm wrestle had to be the person delicately stated to be 'fucking' Jocelyn's husband in the postcard. This fortunate and happy sighting of his client's husband's presumed adulterous companion did not, however, explain who had sent the card and why. It also failed to provide any insight into why one of Oxton's most laid-back and respectable accountants would engage in very public arm wrestling in the centre of Oxton Town with a woman with whom he was allegedly having a secret affair.

17

A T THE VERY moment Geoffrey and Hilda were arm wrestling, the real Sheila Endwhistle was deeply engaged in an animated conversation with Chief Superintendent Charles Morrow. After her unsuccessful attempt to divorce Fred, she had dutifully returned home to continue her life of marital disharmony. Fred had implored her to give him one more chance and repeated that his love for her compelled him to oppose the granting of a divorce decree. A truce was called. Sheila promised no more non-marital sexual adventures. Fred promised no more flatulence. Both kept their promises for about six weeks and then each resumed normal service. It was over twelve months since the court case and both Sheila and Fred were sleeping in separate bedrooms.

The chief superintendent two days earlier had fulfilled a lifetime ambition and become the proud owner of a sparkling new red, top of the range, F-type Jaguar sports car together with its 567 bhp, 'exquisite handling precision and chassis composure' as praised in the car's brochure. The car, fully purchased with various add on extras for a sum of £110,000, was the product of twenty years scrounging and saving as Charles Morrow worked his way up from a lonely street constable walking the beat into the upper echelons of Oxton Town's constabulary. Sheila, somewhat out of sorts and bad humoured as a result of a planned wedding being cancelled, had in a moment of mild distraction while driving along Meadow Road opened her car window and blown a sarcastic wolf whistle at one of the treacherous neighbours who had a year earlier turned up in court as one of Fred's witnesses. Remembering too late the yield sign which brought traffic to a halt at the junction with Clover Avenue, she had belatedly jammed on her brakes and careered into the rear of the chief superintendent's new Jaguar, which had been yielding in dutiful obedience to the roadside instruction.

The impact of Sheila's seven-year-old Toyota Corolla on the sports car resounded down the road with a sound of crunching metal and shattering glass, followed by the explosive opening of the mangled sports car's small boot and the propulsion into the air of a semi-clothed woman taking off like a rocket. Having turned three somersaults worthy of an Olympic gymnast, the flying female then returned to earth with a splat, face down on the Toyota's still surviving windscreen.

Sheila sat paralysed in her seat, staring at the innocent sky blue eyes with long black eyelashes staring down at her and at a gaping hole which had replaced what should have been a nose and mouth. Fighting amidst the wreckage to say something suitable, an 'AARGH' escaped from Sheila's mouth as she stared transfixed at the splattered remains of the young woman she believed she had just murdered and at her various body parts glued to her car's cracked windscreen. The horror and revulsion caused by the sight of two obviously battered and shrivelled legs, one with a foot half cut off, resulted in Sheila staggering out of the wreckage of her pulverised Corolla and depositing her recently eaten lunch all over an enraged Charles Morrow. The chief superintendent had moments earlier climbed out of his battered Jaguar intending to throw the legal book at the lunatic who had just attempted to mow him down. However, the book remained under wraps as Sheila's dramatic car exit and food sharing exploits coincided with Oxton's award-winning policeman spotting with horror what was left of Cynthia, 'The World's Juiciest Hairiest Blow-up Doll' attached to the Corolla's windscreen.

'Oh my god, oh my god, I've killed someone,' Sheila screeched hysterically. 'Call an ambulance, someone call an ambulance, it's too horrible, I didn't mean to do it, it was an accident. Oh my god, I'm a murderer, I'm a murderer,' she howled, tears pouring down her cheeks as she slowly sank to the ground.

As the normally diffident citizens of Oxton in the vicinity started to gather and show some interest in the roadside drama and one or two benevolent concerned stationery pedestrians looked posed to offer help, Charles Morrow desperately tried to silence the verbose motorised maniac as he wiped her vomit off his chin.

'It's only a doll, it's only a doll. For god's sake shut up, you've done enough damage already,' he hissed in as low a voice as possible.

'I've murdered a doll, I've murdered a doll,' Sheila babbled. 'I've murdered a... a... is it only a doll?' she asked, lowering her voice and regaining some but not all of her composure.

'A bloody doll, you lunatic,' Charles Morrow roared at the very moment the Corolla windscreen, suffering the delayed impact of Sheila's motorised meanderings, fortuitously for the superintendent, fell into the car and out of sight together with his beloved Cynthia's fragmented parts.

'I'm very sorry,' said Sheila regaining some composure. 'I was distracted for a moment. It was only a doll, was it?'

'Shush... shush... please don't say any more about that,' Charles Morrow pleaded, a look of desperation on his face, as the crowd of onlookers continued to increase.

'It's alright. No one hurt,' he announced authoritatively to anyone interested, applying his police training and years of experience in assertive crowed control.

'Just a minor accident. As chief super I'll look after it, no need to linger, move along now. Let's not cause another accident. Move along.'

Realising that no one was dead and concluding that nothing further of any major interest was going to happen, the gawkers slowly dispersed as oncoming traffic slowed down, carefully avoiding the mating vehicles and scattered debris. Suffering temporarily from shock, Sheila sat slumped on the roadside kerb repetitively muttering under her breath, 'It's only a doll, it's only a doll,' trying to digest the real significance of what she had just been told.

As the crowd disappeared the chief superintendent removed from the Corolla's wreckage what remained of Cynthia's identifiable parts, which included a pelt of what appeared to be thick black pubic hair sitting on the top of the car's gear stick like a deranged hedgehog. As he did so, a cruising police patrol car stopped by and the driver, Constable Janet Constable, enquired whether help was needed. Constable Constable, having been given a somewhat limited and circumscribed version of events, helpfully called Oxton police station and requested that two trucks be assigned to remove the immobile vehicles to the local garage for repair. That having been promptly arranged with the assistance of Sergeant Benny Sergeant, the patrol car then resumed patrolling as Sergeant Sergeant went about making the necessary arrangements.

In fulfilment of his official duties, Chief Superintendent Morrow noted Sheila's name, address, her car reg and the name of her insurance company. He also checked her driver's licence, which she extricated from the side pocket of a car door. He then hailed a passing taxi and took her to the New York deli for a coffee. Although the victim of Sheila's negligent driving, the chief superintendent felt obliged to further check whether she was well enough to return home or should make a precautionary visit to Oxton Hospital's A&E for a physical examination and some calming medication. He also wanted to ascertain the extent to which Sheila had come to terms with the scattered remains of Cynthia temporarily panicking her into believing that she was about to be charged with murder.

Sitting in the deli, Charles Morrow informed Sheila that he intended to regard the crash solely as a personal civil matter and that she would not be prosecuted under the Road Traffic Acts. This was conditional on her speedily admitting responsibility for the crash to her insurance company so that it would rapidly pay out the funds required to fully repair his newly acquired Jaguar and restore its road worthiness. Unsurprisingly, he made no mention of seeking an insurance sum to compensate for the destruction of Cynthia, his loss of her services or any consequential emotional stress.

'But what about your daughter's doll? I've got to pay for that.'

Sheila responded, reaching seriously mistaken conclusions as to the existence of a daughter and regarding the ownership and function of the dramatically decommissioned adult plaything.

'No, that's not necessary. I'll take personal care of that,' Charles Morrow responded anxious to get off the subject. This markedly contrasted with the anxiety felt immediately prior to the crash. Five minutes before his unscheduled meeting with Sheila, pretending to check the air in his spare tyre, he had secretly inflated Cynthia in Stewart's Garage forecourt as she lay stretched out and airless hidden in the Jaguar's car boot. As he drove out of the garage his main anxiety had been to drive to a suitable private location where he could get on the subject. Despite the chief superintends newly acquired and readily understandable anxiety, Sheila was clearly not going to be put off the subject easily.

'No, I insist I replace the doll. Despite my awful driving you have been very kind. I must,' she insisted.

Charles Morrow momentarily kept his silence. Studying Sheila he considered her offer and concluded that a Sheila substitute for Cynthia had serious potential. He had always wondered what it would be like to play with a really big live doll. A doll that actually walked and talked and didn't have to be surreptitiously pumped up in a garage forecourt on a regular basis. Such a change he reasoned could considerably boost his quality of life and his happiness index. It wasn't easy for a single man of his age who had devoted himself twenty-four seven to his policing duties and public service to continue indefinitely leading a life in which his only female companion was made of rubber. He decided to take the plunge.

'It wasn't my daughter's doll, I don't have a daughter, it

was mine. And... er... it wasn't a normal doll really,' he rapidly explained, immediately regretting his impulsiveness.

'Oh,' Sheila responded, not really understanding why a chief superintendent would have an abnormal doll. 'I'm not sure I know what you mean.'

'Don't worry about it. It's ok,' Charles Morrow replied squirming, suddenly anxious to end the conversation. 'There's no need for you to buy a new one. Please don't worry about it. The important thing is that neither of us is injured. Stuff happens, it could have been much worse.'

He gulped down what was left of his coffee, overcome by a desire to escape from the deli.

'Can you make your own way home or should I join you in a taxi?' he politely enquired, steadying his nerves.

'I'm ok. I think I'll just sit here for a while and recover from all the excitement. I can then get a bus home,' replied Sheila.

'Ok, well I'll be in touch after I have received the garage's repair estimate. I must be off now,' said a fleeing Charles Morrow.

With that he left £10 at the cash desk to pay for the two coffees and hurried out of the deli. As he closed the door behind him the significance of their conversation dawned on Sheila. 'Stuff happens,' she recalled Cyril Braithwaite had said in the courts after her brief description to him of her late-night engagement with her imbibing companions just prior to her divorce case commencing. Now Sheila realised more stuff had just happened.

'Oh, it's one of those sorts of dolls,' she muttered to herself and giggled for the first time since she had accidentally bumped into the officer in command of the local constabulary.

To Sheila Endwhistle the notion of replacing Cynthia was

also quite an attractive proposition. Their unconventional first meeting added an extra frisson of excitement to the concept. She wondered whether the chief super always wore plain clothes or whether he also occasionally wore a uniform. The idea of a uniformed Charles Morrow doing with Sheila what he had obviously previously done with Cynthia was now looming large in Sheila's fantasy of life. After all, a girl is entitled to some fun.

18

CYRIL BRAITHWAITE drove home slowly from his office. The sky was blue, the sun was shining and all would have been well in Cyril's world if he had not had another disturbing visit from Pamela Bull that afternoon. She told Cyril that she had implemented her plan and that for the previous six weeks she had made love with Bart almost every night. Three times he had successfully pleaded for a night off. On occasions the next day was a Sunday, they had spent the day together and there was no opportunity for him to stray elsewhere. She had also regularly called into his office around lunchtime on days when he was not in the courts and taken him off for a variety of pub lunches. As a result, he had little spare time for any desk-top extramarital experimentation. Pamela believed everything was going well when out of the blue that very morning she found another card in an envelope from an anonymous correspondent in her letterbox.

The redhead is still providing the goods

From a friend,

the glued together newsprint on the card read.

'I'm not sure when the goods are provided but I really don't care anymore. I am going to divorce the two-timing bastard,' Pamela told Cyril.

Despite Cyril insisting the card's author could just be a local crank, Pamela insisted that Cyril 'get the divorce ball rolling', threatening to exact excruciating revenge on both of Bart's balls next time they opportunistically became available in the marital bed. To Cyril's relief, after further engagement she agreed to do nothing rash save for instructing Cyril to write to Bart informing him of her intention to issue divorce proceedings.

'You really can't be sure he is being unfaithful,' Cyril cautioned, but as far as Pamela was concerned caution had ceased to be relevant.

'Look, either you send the bastard that letter or I will ask another solicitor to do so,' she roared and then, almost immediately, apologised. 'Look, it's not your fault and I know you may be right but I can't go on as if nothing is wrong. I don't believe anyone, whoever it is, would go to so much trouble to send me these messages if they weren't true. Why bother? Anyway, once Bart has received your letter, he will still have an opportunity to explain himself.'

Cyril agreed to send the letter but was unhappy doing so. Considering the number of crazy people he had met, represented and also defended his clients against, as a solicitor, he had no doubt there were plenty of nut cases with enough spare time on their hands 'to go to so much trouble' without a second thought.

* * *

Joshua Shoshowski sat behind his desk reviewing the progress made so far in solving the anonymous postcard mystery. He had received from each client a list of friends' names. Except for the Geoffrey Brewer midday surveillance he had been totally unsuccessful in discovering any illicit sexual adventures by any of those he had followed. Even Geoffrey could so far only be proved to have engaged in public displays of lunchtime arm wrestling with the person he still mistakenly presumed to be Sheila Endwhistle.

Joshua slowly read through the lists of names to identify any name or names common to each list. Six out of the ten lists received included as a friend the local rector, Peter Howick. A popular clergyman amongst Oxton townsfolk and one not known for excessive moralising, Joshua gave no credence to the possibility that the good rector could be a cause of all the trouble. The hairstylist, Desiree Honeycombe, was mentioned by five of Joshua's clients. Hair stylists, Joshua knew, spend their days listening to gossip and he assumed that Desiree would do nothing that could risk sabotaging her successful business or upsetting her customers, particularly after the over sensationalised front-page story in the Oxton Weekly News reporting the Eldon Pettigrew court hearing. Chief Superintendent Morrow also featured on four lists. From Joshua's knowledge of the chief superintendent's private hobbies, he seemed an unlikely suspect for the conducting of an anonymous crusade to protect Oxton from adulterers. Having checked and cross checked all the lists of 'friends' Joshua realised he was none the wiser. His only conclusion was that either the 'friend' was not a friend at all or that all of his clients had a friend none could recollect.

Joshua acknowledged that he was no closer to identifying the friendly sender of the postal messages. For the sake of appearances and to ensure his clients lost no confidence in his professionalism as a private detective he decided he better be seen to be pursuing some reasonable line of enquiry. If not for the revelation of the contents of his brief case a year earlier, the chief superintendent would have been an obvious suspect. He determined he would keep a close watch on his activities over the next few weeks. Maybe he had suffered a personality change since their last encounter, he mused.

19

I T WAS A SATURDAY afternoon. Oxton Rovers were playing a home match in Oxton Park, their soccer ground. Their Division Two opponents were only two points ahead of them in the football league and Cyril had taken Aloysius off with him to see the match.

The offices of Braithwaite Marshall & Co, as is usual on a Saturday afternoon, were closed and the blinds in Cyril's room were drawn. In the murky darkness the rubber tree stood rooted to the pot silently at peace with itself. It contemplated the events of the week just gone and anticipated the excitement of the week that would shortly dawn. It felt reinvigorated by the arrival of the small Swiss cheese plant purchased by Cyril a few days earlier sitting on the mantlepiece above the gas fireplace. The rubber tree regarded it as a welcome vegetating companion with which it could daily release oxygen, absorb carbon dioxide and help save the planet from humanity's over exploitation, stupidity and neglect. The loneliness of being the law firm's solitary ecological saviour had finally ended.

The rubber tree felt a spurt coming on and stretching its roots, grew a quarter of an inch as a new leaf silently unfurled. If only that idiot would stop putting me to sleep with his self-absorbed boring conversation, I would be at least five inches taller by now and much more environmentally effective, it told itself. It acknowledged that being a rubber tree was a very exacting occupation in a solicitor's office. Not only did it have to listen to an awful lot of rubbish but there was also only limited room for personal expansion. You had to grow a little to retain the waterer's interest but not too much, as otherwise you were at risk of getting too big and of being dumped into the bin. Life was really so complicated. It would be so much easier to be a rubber tree growing in one of the tourist resorts in southern Spain or, better still, along the side of the Amazon river in South America. Oh to be watered regularly with unlimited space to spread your roots and stretch your branches! Things, however, could be worse, it reasoned. It could be stuck in an office full of newly convinced Greens so committed to protecting the global environment and saving the planet that, like its cousin, it would be totally forgotten, pass out from lack of water, lose all its leaves and end its days on the town dump.

A little sunlight slipped through a gap in the blinds and threw its warm rays carelessly onto a table just a foot away from the rubber tree. It felt a rush of excitement as it stood waiting to feel the bright warm glow of the sun on its newly unfurled leaf grown as a welcoming gesture to its new friend, the Swiss cheese plant. As the minute hand of the clock on Cyril's desk moved slowly forward, the sunshine got closer. Just as it was about to kiss the leaves of the rubber tree with its warmth a cloud intervened, moving rapidly across the Oxton sky, hiding the sun and the room once again descended into murky darkness.

A combination of disappointment and mid-afternoon fatigue struck the rubber tree. Falling asleep it missed the day's main office event when twenty minutes later a figure walked swiftly across the room and sat down at Cyril's desk. Turning on and then reading content on his laptop screen, the figure took some shots with a mobile phone, turned off the laptop and then speedily departed. Although spotted by the Swiss cheese plant, there was no danger of betrayal. It was too young to understand and just assumed it was all part of the normal Saturday afternoon office routine. Its main concern was to devise a strategy which would ensure the rubber tree when sleeping, remained silent. Its incoherent mumbling when asleep, audible only to stationary vegetation but obviously inaudible to the strange mobile vegetation that had entered the room and later departed, was starting to drive it crazy. It hoped that one day it also might become mobile and be able to jump off the mantlepiece and plonk itself down in a sunnier and less sound intrusive location!

20

MIRANDA BRAITHWAITE'S twice weekly visits for sessions of self-analysis, self-assertiveness and self-appreciation were having an impact. It was over two years since her father's death, sixty-eight sessions and £34,000 later before she realised, in what her therapist described as a major breakthrough, that she had to stop leading a fantasy existence using soap characters, television series and reality show personalities as role models and return to the real world.

'Analyse your life. Look at how you spend your time,' Dr Norman Zendlove had repetitively urged Miranda during their various engagements. Miranda that afternoon, in a stream of consciousness, enthusiastically and critically portrayed to the psychiatrist the most recent repeated episode of Sally Rooney's Normal People, watched by her the night before on BBC One. 'As they are both intelligent, I don't really understand why Anne Marie and Connell regularly screw, then row and fall out. And they each at times seem so vulnerable and lonely,' she told the therapist, concluding a graphic description of the latest events in the fraught fictional life of the two Trinity College, Dublin undergraduates whose complex relationship and university college life in Ireland the series portrayed.

This unprecedented, astonishingly insightful pronouncement

by Miranda, the first of its kind in her counselling sessions, galvanised Dr Zendlove into action.

'Why do you say that?' he ingeniously asked, deploying the full depth of his nine years' schooling in psychiatry and ten years' practical knowledge as a therapist.

'It's just not right. Surely such intelligent people would talk more to each other about their personal problems and not just let stuff happen?' came the incisive reply.

'Amazing,' commented the good doctor, uncharacteristically deviating from the traditional therapist's role of merely asking questions. He knew that anyone who could critically analyse the graphically described storyline had to have something worthwhile to offer beyond merely viewing more of the same. The real problem, he knew, looking at Miranda, was to figure out exactly what it was she had to offer other than a head filled with televisual nonsense decorated by fictitious social media stories and a body that gave him a hard on every time she lay on his couch.

'I think, doc,' continued the patient, 'I'm growing out of watching this stuff. I can't spend the rest of my life as a couch potato. I want some fun for myself.'

All the textbooks on psychiatry teach the principle that by asking questions the psychiatrist or therapist can assist a patient to find the true answer to whatever the problem is that caused the patient to seek help. This approach has a variety of merits. It ensures a never-ending stream of questions can be asked at an ongoing number of hourly chargeable sessions for an unspecified period of time. A good psychiatrist can ask a range of questions and sound authoritative whilst not being obliged to express any opinion of any nature whatsoever and without having to give any prognosis or guidance on how the problem, whatever it is, might cease impacting on the patient paying to be interrogated. If the psychiatrist runs out of questions, it is not only permissible but also desirable to revisit again all of the original questions to check the truth and accuracy of the original answers to ensure they are awarefully introspective. If different answers are given the second time around, a third series of the same questions is then required to identify which of the replies given are true and can constructively contribute to the patient's better mindfulness. It, of course, doesn't really matter which version of events or description of personal feelings is actually true because what impacts on the patient is his or her perception of their truth even where their truth is a pack of lies. Even that doesn't really matter because no psychiatrist ever has any totally reliable strategies and anything more than tentative answers to resolve any patient's problems. However, attempting to identify what is true satisfies any personal curiosity about a patient's background, keeps the bank manager happy and ensures that both the patient and the psychiatrist each feel they are using their time productively and the patient that she or he is getting some value for consulting fees paid.

The concept of Miranda wanting 'fun for herself' was linked in Dr Zendlove's mind with the concept of personal expansion which he believed it was his duty to transmit to his patients to enable them to broaden their horizons and perspective on life. As Miranda innocently, and in his mind seductively, stretched out on his couch, Dr Zendlove was affected by an unexpected glitch in the transmission process. It was he, not his patient, who had entered a state of personal expansion.

Miranda paused for breath at the end of yet another stream of consciousness and Norman Zendlove remained unusually silent. For the first time ever, his brain froze as another anatomical part involuntarily hardened. Without prior warning, he threw caution and all psychiatric principles to the wind, plonked his glasses on to his coffee table, dropped his trousers to the floor and spat his pipe out as he spontaneously launched himself through the air, a poor imitation of a falling high wire trapeze artist, intent on landing on top of Miranda. A moment later the airborne therapists adventure came to an abrupt, startling and appropriate end when his trouser leg became entangled around the chair on which he had been sitting and his over sensitised hardened part accompanied by an unusual screeching sound crashed into the side of the analyst's couch, immediately prior to the good doctor blacking out. Miranda, eyes closed, in a partially hypnotised state of relaxation, lay still awaiting the next question, and when it failed to materialise peacefully fell asleep. She was happily oblivious to the unconscious remnants of an analytical mind that lay crumpled on the floor beside her.

21

C YRIL WAS HAVING another one of those days. It was
11 a.m. on a Monday morning and a weeping Jemima
Hardcastle sat in his office for what Ethel insensitively described
as an emergency consultation on an issue of deadly importance.
Her mother had died the previous Friday and Jemima told Cyril
that the funeral was scheduled for Oxton Cemetery in four days'
time.

'It is all so upsetting,' said the tearful client. 'I found her body
when visiting her home late Friday afternoon. She was stone cold
dead. There was an autopsy over the weekend. I was told a chicken
bone was found stuck in her throat that she must have swallowed
that day when eating her lunch. She choked, collapsed and died.
All alone. Had I visited three hours earlier I could have tried the
Hymie manoeuvre and maybe saved her.'

'Oh, that's very upsetting,' responded Cyril, presenting his
sensitive side and ignoring the 'Hymie' reference. He attributed
to stress her mentioning a manoeuvre with a man, likely Jewish,
named Hymie as a semantically confused reference to the
Heimlich manoeuvre. Whilst the inventor of the life saving
manoeuvre, Henry Heimlich, born in Wilmington, Delaware, in
the USA, was in fact the Jewish son of Mary (Epstein) and Philip
Heimlich. Cyril doubted Henry's parents or friends ever called

him Hymie and that Jemima knew the inventor of the manoeuvre was Jewish. Cyril only knew this as he had read Henry Heimlich's obituary in the Guardian newspaper following his death in December 2016.

'But how can I help,' Cyril asked, refocusing, hoping Jemima didn't want him to sue the butcher or the owner of the chicken farm or worse still, what remained of the corpse of the cooked dead chicken.

'The problem is the manager of the cemetery is refusing to bury my mother with my father,' Jemima explained.

'Oh, did he also just die?' asked Cyril wondering which parent died first or whether her father was so grief stricken that he had dropped dead after Jemima discovered her late mother's body.

'No, no, the bastard died three years ago,' Jemima delicately explained. 'The problem is he and my mum twenty years ago agreed they would both be buried in the same cemetery plot that he purchased. He deserted my mum ten years ago and went off with a dolly bird. Mum kept the family home after he died. It was purchased in their joint names and after his death she became the sole owner but he had no other assets or savings other than the burial plot. When I called the cemetery manager to arrange for the plot to be reopened for Mum's burial he said there was a problem.'

'What's the problem?' asked Cyril.

'He has a letter on file from the dolly bird, Helen Gravelawn, stating she is the executor and sole beneficiary of my late dad's estate, instructing that the grave should not be reopened before her death and that hers is the only other body that can be laid to rest in it.'

'But if he deserted your mum years ago, why does that matter? Can't your poor mum be buried in an alternative grave in the cemetery?' asked Cyril, looking confused and struggling to cope with the 'dolly bird's' coincidentally odd surname.

'Well, she could but I want to fulfil her wishes. She told me that she was determined to catch up with the bastard one day and make his life miserable. She also asked to ensure she is buried on top of him. If there really is an afterlife, she wants to be up close and personal.'

'So this is about a possible afterlife? Is that it?' enquired Cyril, who believed his daily life sufficiently bizarre without having to delve into the hereafter.

'Well not just that,' confessed Jemima. 'I want to stick it to her, the Gravelawn woman. I really like the idea of my mum putting one over on her as her final act in this world. Her burial on top of my dad will cause her no end of grief.'

'Ah, so your objective is not only to fulfil your mum's wishes but also revenge, is that a fair comment?' asked Cyril, hoping he was not putting his two feet in it.

'I suppose so,' admitted Jemima. 'As my mum wanted to be laid to rest in the same plot I am determined she gets her way and Gravelawn's grave stealing is totally buried. So Mr Braithwaite, legally what can be done?'

'Give me a couple of hours to think it over and then come back around 3 p.m. for another consultation. I haven't come across this problem before. Do I have your permission to talk to both Johnny Bleak, the cemetery manager and Rector Peter Howick?' asked Cyril.

'Sure, go ahead. Thank you for meeting me so quickly,' said

Jemima, who then stood up, gratefully shook Cyril's outstretched hand and left his office.

* * *

'So here's the thing. Ms Gravelawn has no legal authority to stop the cemetery from re-opening my client's father's plot and preventing her mother's burial in it,' asserted Cyril.

'I sympathise, I really do. Unfortunately, Mr Braithwaite I don't think you are right. Our records show that the father paid for the plot, said nothing about it being jointly purchased with the deceased and that Ms Gravelawn, named as his sole executor and beneficiary in his will, inherited whatever property he owned when he died. The will was never challenged and it is clear that the plot, as his sole asset, is now owned by the Gravelawn woman. If I defy her instructions the cemetery board could be sued and would be at risk of having to pay her damages. There would also be a major risk of her later obtaining a court order that the mother's body be exhumed and planted, er sorry, buried elsewhere.'

Having been emailed a copy of Jemima's father's will Cyril couldn't argue with Johnny Bleak's legal logic, recognising he had specialist legal expertise on the topic of wills and burials. Their conversation had ended on a friendly note when he informed Cyril that on previous occasions a similar problem had arisen and he was sorry he could not be more helpful.

Next stop was a conversation with Rector Peter Howick, with whom he ate a ham and salad sandwich and drank a lunchtime cup of coffee in Oxton's New York deli.

'I am sure God would want them buried together and rejoined in matrimony but, unfortunately, on this earth mammon is frequently more powerful than God,' he regretfully exclaimed.

'Ah,' said Cyril, 'but doesn't God sometimes work in mysterious ways? There must be a way of solving this.'

'Maybe there is. I will pray and perhaps one of us will have a helpful revelation.'

'Maybe,' replied a cynical Cyril. The pair then went on to discuss Oxton Rovers stunning unexpected 6–0 victory on Saturday, which the rector insisted was achieved with God's help. What other explanation could be given for two of their opponent's players being sent off by the referee before half time, one for inadvertently spitting as Oxton's centre forward ran past resulting in the spittle getting accidentally embedded up the centre forward's right nostril. Gary Lineker had on BBC One's Match of the Day excitedly pronounced the 'shocking' spittle incident as a global soccer first not to be sniffed at and destined to feature in the record books. In the background members of the programmes production crew could be heard hysterically laughing, a BBC first.

After lunching with the rector Cyril slowly walked back to his office deep in thought. He had no idea what to say to Jemima Hardcastle at three o'clock. As he walked he overheard two people passing by discussing a cremation they had attended that very morning in Oxton's crematorium, located close to Oxton Cemetery. Unexpectedly, his faith in divine revelation was restored.

* * *

'I think I've solved your problem,' Cyril said to Jemima, who was sitting on the edge of her seat by the coffee table in Cyril's office.

'What is important to you, to use your phrase, is that your late mum is laid to rest on top of your deceased father and that the Gravelawn women doesn't stop that happening. Am I right?'

'Yes, you've got it in one.'

'Well instead of continuing a row with the cemetery manager that we can't win, why not sidestep the problem and totally undermine Ms Gravelawn's heartless stance. If you have no principled objection, instead of burying your mum in the grave with your dad, how about cremating her body and sprinkling her ashes on top of his grave, mingled with some soil so they are invisible. Afterwards you can ensure Ms Gravelawn is told, but there will be nothing she can do about it.'

Jemima Hardcastle sat quietly for a couple of minutes gravely thinking and Cyril remained seated, eagerly awaiting her response. She then, for the first time since her mother's death, smiled broadly.

'I think you've cracked it, Mr Braithwaite. Brilliant. Everyone says you are great in solving unusual problems. Before I saw you this morning I met the town undertakers but they were totally clueless. Ever considered expanding your office business to include undertaking?' she enquired.

'No, I think what I do is unusual enough. I prefer working with the living than the dead,' Cyril responded, while silently acknowledging that too frequently he had to advise the brain dead.

'Thank you so much. How much do I owe you?' asked the grateful bereaved.

'Nothing, just attribute the solution to divine revelation,' answered Cyril, surprising himself with his generosity and a temporary belief in God. 'Just one thing, I want to be invited to the sprinkling of the ashes, which I suggest takes place without fanfare, quietly after dark. We must all then retire to the Ancient Wig to celebrate your mother's life. The cemetery's gates have been stuck open for over two years and are never locked. So gaining access will not be a problem. The next day, if you wish, I will send a letter to Ms Gravelawn on your behalf protesting her insensitivity and informing her of the location of the ashes.'

'Problem solved then,' remarked Ethel Edelwitz after the departure of the clearly satisfied client.

'Another burning issue dead and almost buried,' remarked an unusually chipper Cyril. Later that evening when driving to the Ancient Wig for his nightly pint he phoned the rector and asked that he join him. He owed him one in recognition of the value of prayer and to thank him for God's work. For once Cyril agreed that God truly works in mysterious ways.

22

'Yo, good to see you!' exclaimed Hilda as Geoffrey Brewer entered the New York deli for an early lunch.

'Hiya Hilda,' responded Geoffrey, no longer entirely committed to the King's English. 'How's it going?'

'Everything's going good, real good,' she replied.

They sat down together and ordered. Geoffrey had by now been conditioned into unashamedly staring at her prominent breasts and Hilda enjoyed checking his below the waist bulge. They had been meeting lunchtime, Monday to Friday for eight weeks in a row. 'Heavy rapping' and 'talking dirty', as Hilda described it, had become for Geoffrey a new lunchtime pastime. Thinking dirty had also taken his mind at lunchtime off his clients' concerns.

Geoffrey sat entranced by Hilda's provocative body movements and excessively stimulating conversation as he sexually hyperventilated. Hilda had explained that although he really turned her on, she would love to feel his large smooth hands slowly stroking her naked body and she wanted to give him a good time, she couldn't for another seven months. Her husband, Maurie, had died in a car crash only five months earlier. Although she hadn't greatly mourned the dim schmuck's passing, neither his business achievements nor his lovemaking attributes having added up to much, she was sticking to the family tradition of one year's celibacy from the date of his death out of respect for the dead. She felt he deserved at least some respect for the one outstanding business investment of his life, that is his investment in his own death. Just eleven days prior to his becoming a no-fault victim in a fatal road traffic accident he had taken out a life policy for £3.8 million naming Hilda as sole beneficiary. This sum, together with the expected monetary damages that her solicitor advised she would receive from the company that had insured the articulated lorry which had ploughed through the deceased's dark blue 1980s Volkswagen Golf, would leave her financially secure for life.

Deli arm wrestling was the only form of physical contact Hilda allowed Geoffrey and their eccentric lunchtime jousts had become a source of daily amusement to the deli's patrons. Many believed that they were actors employed by the deli's manager to create a New York deli style atmosphere. Despite being abandoned by Hilda at the end of every lunch to sexual self-fulfillment, Geoffrey persisted with their odd liaison as it enabled him to temporarily escape from what Jocelyn criticised as his boring, sedate, rustic approach to life and accountant's mindset. His unconventional encounters with Hilda had created a frisson of excitement and anticipation not previously experienced and he enjoyed the novelty. She not only gave him a lunchtime hard on but also brought a new bounce to his step. However, while Geoffrey desperately aspired to a little bit of adultery and was willing to wait a few months to fulfil his aspiration, he did not want to become a divorce statistic. Like many men, he wanted to have his cake while eating another with a different icing on top!

Unknown to Geoffrey his lunchtime meetings with Hilda had continued to be monitored by an increasingly puzzled Joshua Shoshowski, who after observing two months of public arm wrestling felt the pressure to report some positive progress to Bartholomew Bull for the benefit of at least one of his clients. A few days later a report accompanied by a selection of illustrative photographs arrived in the offices of Moore Bull & Co stating that Mr Geoffrey Brewer was engaging in public lunchtime acts of sado-masochism in Oxton's New York deli with a woman known as Hilda whose real name he believed to be Sheila Endwhistle. He hoped shortly to be able to provide additional background and other relevant particulars.

23

THE ENVELOPE WAS marked 'Private & Confidential – to be opened by Bartholomew Bull ONLY'. Despite the falling out, Cyril did not want to cause any unnecessary upset to the staff and partners of his first solicitor's firm and was personally sceptical of the anonymised warnings Pamela Bull had received. If they were untrue, he did not want Bartholomew Bull's secretary, Cindy Bretson, to open a letter alleging she was engaged in an action replay with her boss of the fatal antics of Cyril's deceased present partner who just happened to be Bartholomew's deceased former partner. Cyril appreciated that the unusual linkage between their two firms had proved a valuable source of revenue to him and wished to avoid causing more upset than was inevitable.

Bartholomew Bull, at fifty years of age, was physically the exact opposite of his deceased former partner. Ten years his junior, he weighed in at 163 pounds, was six feet one inch tall and of slender build with a full mop of straight brown hair. A health freak, he jogged five miles every morning, summer and winter, before work and at day's end he worked out with weights in his office before showering and then driving home. A healthy body guarantees an alert and healthy mind, he would tell any client who gazed quizzically at the unusual selection of dumbbells that adorned the walls along the side of his office floor. He was proud that the law firm in which he was the senior partner was not only the leading firm in Oxton Town but was also recognised as one of the major law firms in the County of Herbitshire.

Most of Bartholomew's day was filled with company formations, business law and the buying and selling of business and residential properties. Until Michael Marshall's death he had never dealt with divorce law but over the previous two years a number of the town's leading citizens had specifically requested his advice and assistance to resolve their matrimonial conflicts. As the economy was in deep recession and the number of lucrative house sales had dramatically fallen, he had taken up dealing with family problems.

A monogamous man of conservative disposition, totally devoted to his wife Pamela, Bartholomew had initially been 'somewhat disturbed' by some of the more sordid stories of marital infidelity and violence on which he had given advice. 'Somewhat disturbed' was the euphemism used by him in conversation with other legal luminaries over a pint in the Ancient Wig. A similar description had previously been applied by him to his reaction to discovering the predilections of the late Michael Marshall. A more truthful and vivid description would have been 'completely unhinged', the reality being that the unusual circumstances of MM's death had temporarily undermined the sanity of both of his surviving legal partners. While Jonathan Moore had by now completely recovered, some of Bartholomew's hinges had continued to hang loose. They were now permanently disabled due to his being verbally force-fed a continuing diet of marital adventurism he had previously never suspected to be an integral part of daily life in the sedate rural setting of Oxton Town.

While Bartholomew Bull believed that he had adapted well to becoming a family law practitioner and learnt to cope both with the emotional stress of advising Oxton's Kama Sutra devotees and the negative publicity surrounding Michael Marshall's unexpected demise, no other member of the legal profession in the entire County of Herbitshire shared that belief. All the other legal eagles, except his surviving partner, thought Bartholomew had lost some vital lawyering ingredient. Some simply thought he had lost it altogether.

24

CINDY BRETSON HAD long red hair, large pinkish freckles all over her face which she unsuccessfully tried to hide behind Lancôme's most expensive bronze moisturiser, big green eyes and a body that made fat women weep and old men stare. Unknown to Bartholomew Bull she had found him attractive on the very first occasion they had met at her successful job interview. It was her attraction to him which had resulted in her agreeing to her employment as his secretary despite offers on the same day of alternative employment at a higher salary by two other potential employers.

The bizarre and tragic death of Marybelle Brown had occurred only a short time before the commencement of Cindy's employment in Moore Bull & Co. A more demanding unionised employee intent on asserting her rights, committed to ensuring that workers were not unfairly exploited or sexually harassed by their bosses and supportive of the #MeToo movement would have been alerted by this bizarre event to the unexpectedly hazardous nature of her job contract, which stated that she was 'employed to work under the senior partner, Bartholomew Bull' and would have demanded additional compensation (that is, a wage hike) to remain Bartholomew's secretary. This did not cross Cindy's mind as, also unknown to Bartholomew, she was fixated by fantasies about his hidden but obviously impressive biceps.

The trauma of the office deaths hung over everyone in the firm in the months that followed. It was only after the first anniversary had passed without an illustrated retrospective appearing in the local Oxton Weekly News that the atmosphere settled down and weeks went by without them being a topic of conversation between clients and the firm's partners and employees. During this time Cindy prioritised being as supportive as possible to Bartholomew in his daily work. She believed this not only required carrying out his instructions correctly and promptly but also, on occasion, taking initiatives that eased his burden or enhanced the business of the legal practice. She was delighted that her phone discussion with the financially troubled Oxton Weekly News had proved effective.

Ten days before the anniversary of the firm's unhappy event she had been the recipient of a phone call from a reporter at the paper seeking an off-the-record briefing of its impact on the firm and tittle tattle about both Moore and Bull. Diplomatically telling the reporter to fuck off, she then phoned the paper's editor to remind him solicitors could advertise and to seek a quote for a two-page advert by Moore Bull & Co describing the excellent services offered to the town folks containing a brief complimentary profile of the firm's partners. The editor, who was very glad to oblige, calculated the cost of an illustrated two pager at £8,000 and was too shrewd to ignore Cindy's offhand comment that the firm had determined to let a year pass from Mr Marshall's death before advertising, as it was felt that there was no point in spending such large sums of money when his death was still a major topic of local gossip. Ten minutes after

Cindy's phone call, a three-page illustrated retrospective on the sensational death one year earlier of one of Oxton's leading lawyers to be included in that coming Friday's edition was scrapped. Instead, the pages were devoted to multiple pictures of cats and dogs taken the previous weekend at the Oxton Saturday dog and Sunday cat show together with the winners' proud owners. Inundated in the days that followed by letters to the editor from dedicated readers commenting on the visual similarity between the winning animals and their smiling owners the editor was then confronted by the unexpected dilemma of whether to publish some of the letters for entertainment value or to ignore them all to avoid causing offence and creating the risk of a defamation suit. After a sleepless night he went for publication and be damned, concluding the owners would be so happy to have their pets publicised as winners, it was unlikely they would be offended by their personalised depiction. What he failed to understand was that the owners were so besotted by their animals they were delighted to learn that many in the town had determined they were visually related to them! This confirmed to some that their loved pet really was a long-deceased relation who had reappeared on earth in a different guise.

Cindy understood that the firm's fraught history required that her relationship with Bartholomew remain totally platonic. She did not believe that after all the emotional trauma he would be able to cope with anything more complicated. Bartholomew regarded Cindy as a marvellous support. On occasions when his wife, Pamela, did not call into the office to accompany him to lunch, he brought Cindy with him to the Ancient Wig, innocently adding fuel to the town gossip about the secretarial services the partners in Moore Bull & Co demanded from their staff.

The lunches were arranged with the best of intentions. Bartholomew enjoyed Cindy's company, found he could share with her his worries and also confidentially discuss with her his astonishment at some of the goings on in which his marital clients were engaged. He could not discuss his clients curious philandering with Pamela as not only in doing so would he breach solicitor-client confidentiality he also knew that due to Pamela's sensitivities he would cause her unnecessary distress and embarrassment. Cindy Bretson, he believed, was more worldly than Pamela and, of course, already familiar with some of the details from her work in the firm. Unknown to Bartholomew, the detailed explicit accounts of his clients' activities that he dictated for Cindy to type were as disturbing to Cindy as they were to him. Cindy's dysfunctional grasp of reality was rapidly becoming as unhinged as his own.

* * *

Over seventy per cent of the emails and letters that Bartholomew received from clients were marked 'Private and Confidential' despite the contents of most of them containing information of no major importance or of less intimate detail than was revealed in the narratives contained in the online folders typed by Cindy. Part of her early morning office duties was to open and sort the firm letters received for Bartholomew, run off hard copies of emails in his inbox and then separate them all into various categories of importance.

The in-tray marked 'URGENT' contained all letters enclosing

cheques to discharge fees, lodge money on account or emails confirming the direct transfer of funds to the firm. The tray marked 'VERY IMPORTANT' contained all communications, including court documents that had to be dealt with within a week. The tray marked 'IMPORTANT' contained all communications that could wait a week but that must be dealt with within a month. The tray marked 'NOT URGENT' contained everything else, including commercial flyers, begging letters and promotions. It also contained written or emailed abuse from former clients or losers in court cases the firm had won. About once every six weeks the last tray was turned over on Bartholomew's desk to be dealt with or disposed of into the office bin or shredder.

Unknown to Bartholomew, Cindy also kept locked in her office filing cabinet a fifth in-tray entitled 'MURDER.' It contained threatening communications explicitly describing various imaginative acts of physical damage with which the author, most times anonymous, threatened Bartholomew. Occasionally the author self-identified or was readily identifiable, frequently being a husband Bartholomew got barred from the family home for physical or mental abuse of his wife or a dissatisfied client, previously represented by him, who lost a court case having been exposed as giving untruthful evidence when cross-examined in court.

Confronted that morning by Cyril Braithwaite's 'Private & Confidential – To be opened by Bartholomew Bull ONLY' letter, Cindy, having read it, had to resolve the unexpected dilemma of deciding how to best categorise it, in which tray to place it or whether she should simply hand it to her boss as being in a separate category all of its own. Cindy determined to take time out for reflection over a hot cup of tea. She also wanted time to digest the unfairly spurious and somewhat embarrassing allegations contained in it. If only they were true, she mused, life would be so much more interesting.

25

THE REHABILITATED, re-mechanised and re-energised Jaguar sports car containing Sheila Endwhistle and Chief Superintendent Morrow sped its way along the narrow country roads leading away from Oxton Town in the direction of Oxton Woods. It was ten weeks since they had accidentally bumped into each other, and their unplanned introduction was recalled affectionately by each of them. Within a week of the crash Sheila's insurance company had coughed up a sufficient compensatory sum to ensure the chief superintendents car looked sparklingly new and was fully roadworthy.

Receipt of the cheque, together with a note from Sheila repeating her apologies for her 'brutal driving' and inviting him to join her for a drink so that she could personally thank him for not bringing criminal charges against her, prompted them again meeting. She also wanted to thank him for the efficiency and kindness of Sergeant Sergeant in arranging for her own car to be speedily delivered to her own garage for repair. A spot of lunch was arranged in the Boar's Head, an imaginatively named pub one mile outside Oxton Town. To many of its regulars the pub was also known as the Bores Head, due to the landlord being well known for droning on interminably whenever the subject of Oxton Rovers last match came up in conversation.

For their first planned meeting Sheila wore the same low-cut top that had eighteen months earlier so distracted Cyril during her first consultation with him. The sight of Sheila wearing her revealing ensemble displaying anatomical parts which had earlier that week been the subject of Charles Morrow's night-time fantasies and an unexpected nocturnal emission confirmed the chief superintendent's perception that Sheila could very ably replace the irreparable Cynthia. A man well known throughout Herbitshire constabulary for his decisiveness, he instantly silently acknowledged that Sheila would be a far superior companion than his pliable recently demised love toy or any new substitute. Instead of travelling in the boot of his car she could keep him company sitting in the passenger seat and actively participate in conversation. Monologue would be replaced by dialogue and both orally and physically they could engage in a form of mutual intercourse that had previously proved impossible. Sheila, unlike Cynthia, could provide real sound effects during a bit of nookie and he would no longer be dependent on the continuous playing on a loop of 'Je t'aime', the erotic 1969 amorous pop hit sung by Jane Birkin and Serge Gainsbourg. Even more importantly he could stop worrying that if he moved too quickly while lying on top of any Cynthia successor she might deflate or even burst. Having to pull into a garage and surreptitiously check her air when driving home and washing her down to ensure she remained in good nick would all be a thing of his past.

All in all, Charles Morrow considered meeting Sheila fortuitous. Like all men thinking with their penis he gave no thought to any possible downside dangers to their developing liaison. The fact that he did not give a moment's thought to

Joshua Shoshowski during all of this was understandable, as he had not encountered Joshua since his last court appearance well over a year earlier. The fact that he was not concerned that Fred Endwhistle, Sheila's husband, might discover their liaison was less comprehensible despite Sheila's assurance that he knew nothing of their meeting in the Boar's Head nor their subsequent weekly drives into Oxton Woods for a midday sojourn with nature. The fact that he gave no consideration to the dangers posed to his health by the possibility that when Sheila assumed her favoured 'rodeo' position on top of him to, as she put it, 'ride him like a bucking bronco', her weight might cause him serious physical injury was incomprehensible, taking into account the well-publicised exploits of the late Michael Marshall and his investigation into the solicitor's death.

In the best traditions of the Herbitshire constabulary at no stage during their relationship did Charles Morrow, chief superintendent, policeman of twenty years standing, only five foot seven inches in height and some 140 pounds heavy consider the dangers posed to his physical wellbeing by the possibility that on one of their meetings deep in Oxton Woods, in a moment of high passion, Sheila Endwhistle, now weighing in at 294 pounds might, when on top, accidentally turn their love making into a passionately terminal experience. For the time being, Charles Morrow was happy with his lot, firmly convinced that in both his work and his leisure activities the best was yet to come. As for Sheila, she was happy to have found a small man in uniform to totally dominate. She liked them smaller than her, helpless and at least a little bit squashed!

* * *

'How come,' mused Joshua Shoshowski out loud, having followed the copulating pair one afternoon to Oxton Woods, 'that the chief super is doing his thing with a woman called Sheila Endwhistle when she is anonymously accused of doing her thing with Geoffrey Brewer? Why is it,' he continued silently musing, 'that the person I have now identified as definitely being Sheila Endwhistle, after following her drive from her home to meet up in a car park with the chief super, bears no resemblance to the person I previously presumed to be Sheila Endwhistle in my report to Moore Bull & Co a few days ago? And more importantly, if the lunchtime deli arm wrestler was not Sheila Endwhistle, who was she and why has she been accused of being Sheila Endwhistle and by whom? Did the "whom" simply have it in for Sheila Endwhistle or for Geoffrey Brewer or for both of them?

'Could it be,' he asked himself, 'that in Oxton Town there are two entirely different, unrelated women, both engaged in adulterous exploits, each of whom is coincidently named Sheila Endwhistle? Could it be there isn't a single anonymous postal correspondent but a whole gaggle of them? Is there an epidemic of anonymous postal warriors conspiring to accuse townsfolk of illicit sexual adventure and also an epidemic of women named Sheila Endwhistle engaged in daily debauchery?' Joshua was determined to find out what the hell was going on.

By the end of the week, as a result of further lucrative investigative work, Joshua had managed to answer some of his own questions. He learnt of Sheila's unsuccessful attempt to divorce Fred from a fortuitous drinking session with Fred in the lounge bar of Joshua's local, the Cherry Tree. It became clear that Fred was blissfully ignorant of Sheila's current policing connection, whilst obviously now regretting his successful opposition to her divorce application. Describing his home life as resembling a Trumpian mad house, he complained that although he and Sheila were sleeping apart in different bedrooms and for over six months had been barely on speaking terms, until relatively recently she had still insisted on nightly servicing with what she referred to as her 'conjugals'.

'Seeing as how you wouldn't let me go, you can now bloody well do your duty,' she had apparently told Fred three days after the failed divorce case. And to ensure Fred could do his duty, each night she supervised his swallowing a Viagra tablet with a glass of water two hours before retiring to the bedroom. 'I am a victim of male rape,' Fred bitterly complained to Joshua. As for the arm wrestler, true to what she had told Geoffrey Brewer, Joshua discovered she lived in a nice semi-detached in Dorchester Avenue and was a recently bereaved wealthy widow still officially mourning the death of her over-insured deceased husband. Joshua did not know whether her unconventional lunchtime exploits were a product of her upbringing in Queens, New York or of stress caused by the traumatic premature death of her husband. The truth is he did not care. He now knew the real identity of Geoffrey Brewer's lunchtime companion and could furnish an updated report to Moore Bull & Co. Unfortunately, before he did so, Bartholomew, under pressure from Jocelyn Brewer, arranged for a letter to be hand-delivered for Geoffrey's personal attention to his office marked 'Urgent & Confidential'.

26

GEOFFREY BREWER could hear the 'thump, thump' sound of his racing heart as he read for the tenth time that morning the unexpected letter received from Moore Bull & Co.

Dear Mr Brewer,

We have been consulted by your wife, who informs us you are engaged in an adulterous relationship with one Sheila Endwhistle. The very fact of this relationship is, of itself, a cause of great distress to our client. Your flaunting it by publicly engaging on a daily basis in midday acts of sado-masochism in Oxton Town's New York deli has added to our client's stress and humiliation. If within seven days of this date you do not vacate the family home and confirm your agreement to the granting of a divorce decree, contentious divorce proceedings will issue without further notice. The issuing of such proceedings will be immediately followed by an emergency court application for an expulsion order which, no doubt, will receive the usual headline treatment in the Oxton Weekly News.

It is both our client's and this firm's earnest hope that matters will be amicably resolved and that such course of action will not prove necessary.

Yours faithfully,

Bartholomew Bull

Since receipt of the letter Geoffrey's normal sedate thought processes and relaxed demeanour had disintegrated and he was totally distracted by a confused jumble of unanswered questions. The coherent ones among them included: Why had Jocelyn arranged for the letter to be delivered to him without first saying something? Who the hell was Sheila Endwhistle? Why did Jocelyn think he was engaged in sado-masochistic acts with her in the New York deli? Why did the letter not mention Hilda? How could arm wrestling in a deli be perceived as engaging in public sado-masochism?

Geoffrey had enjoyed the daily midday jousts with Hilda (or should it be Sheila, he wondered) but he had never got near to committing adultery as opposed to merely thinking adultery. Recognising the seriousness of his dilemma he determined he had no choice but to seek advice from Cyril Braithwaite, the only other recognised specialist divorce lawyer in the town. Some time ago he had unsuccessfully attempted to make an appointment with Braithwaite to ask that he represent him on a minor speeding charge before the local magistrates' court. After a bizarre conversation with a demented telephone receptionist, he had abandoned the attempt and successfully represented himself. The charge was dismissed without penalty on condition that he did not again come before the court on a road traffic violation for a full two years. Silently praying to himself that the telephonic terrorist had simply been the berserk meanderings of a seriously dysfunctional algorithm embedded in an automated telephone answering system he slowly and somewhat fearfully phoned Braithwaite Marshall & Co, doubting whether his already jangled nerves could withstand a verbal onslaught similar to the one he had previously experienced.

Much to Geoffrey's relief and surprise his phone call was treated with civility. Two hours later he was sitting opposite Cyril in his office after the receptionist, who identified herself as Ethel, had instantly offered him an emergency appointment with Cyril and explained to him upon his arrival the need to lodge a retainer fee of £10,000 for Cyril's expert services. Instead of placing any obstacles in his path, she emphasised when he phoned the importance of him getting advice that day. Geoffrey had an eerie feeling that she had expected his call but he knew that was impossible. £10,000 lighter he was now sitting opposite Cyril in a murky consultation room, much smaller than his own, strangely dominated by an overgrown rubber tree that was blocking out the light.

'You've never heard of Sheila Endwhistle but you do arm wrestle with a Hilda Hessleberg,' Cyril slowly repeated in his matter-of-fact voice, carefully saying nothing about his own previous legal entanglements with Sheila shortly after the formation and opening of Braithwaite Marshall & Co. He assumed there could not be two Sheila Endwhistles in the town. Perhaps she has changed her name to Hilda Hessleberg, he speculated.

'What about the allegation of adultery with Sheila, or is it Hilda?' he asked.

'I have never touched any part of her body, that is Hilda's body, other than her hand publicly on top of the table? How can that add up to adultery?' asked a clearly frazzled Geoffrey.

'But you didn't tell your wife about these midday meetings. Why was that?' Cyril asked, ignoring his distraught client's questions.

'I don't know. I suppose because she wouldn't have understood. I'm not sure I understand it. It was just different. I had never been, sort of, picked up before. It was a novelty. Even though we only ever met in the deli and did nothing sexual, at least not together... er... with each other, I suppose I felt guilty and knew Jocelyn would disapprove. Oh, Mr Braithwaite, I don't want a divorce, I don't want to move out of my home and I don't want to lose Jocelyn.'

Geoffrey Brewer, who rarely did anything rash, except in the deli with Hilda Hessleberg, and never made impulsive decisions, was surprised by his own spontaneous decisiveness. Until receipt of the letter, he had fantasised about leaving Jocelyn for Hilda and a variety of mutually satisfying activities that rendered arm wrestling obsolete. Now his entire focus was on remaining at home with Jocelyn. His uncharacteristic emotional outburst over, Geoffrey temporarily retreated into accountancy mode. Then filled with horror by the sudden realisation that his daily lunchtime exploits had become a local spectator sport and probable source of endless gossip, he disintegrated in front of Cyril.

'Oh my god,' he wailed, 'Jocelyn must have seen us without telling me. Who else saw us? What if some of my clients were in the deli? What would they think? They might leave me and go to another firm. Oh Mr Braithwaite, what am I going to do? How could I have been so stupid?'

A woman bursting into tears was something Cyril could handle. It fitted neatly into his lifetime's education and role model expectations. A man was more difficult to come to terms with. Some men had cried previously in Cyril's office over the possibility their wives might leave them. Others had cried over the possibility their wives would not leave them. An accountant crying over the possible loss of clients was something entirely new. Words of comfort about the possible loss of a husband or a wife were relatively easy. Words of comfort and consolation about the possible loss of tax clients and their fees were more difficult. Perhaps, Cyril thought, the clients who saw the show would regard Geoffrey Brewer as much better equipped to persuasively wrestle with Inland Revenue on their behalf? Overcome by unaccustomed tact and diplomacy, Cyril restrained himself from immediately sharing this particular insight with Geoffrey, thinking it preferable to share it with the rubber tree after Geoffrey's departure.

Rapidly he brought the consultation to a close on the basis that Cyril would make direct contact with Bartholomew Bull to inform him of Geoffrey's wish that his marriage to Jocelyn remain intact. At the same time a conciliatory replying letter was to be sent denying adultery and stating Geoffrey was agreeable to attending marriage counselling with Jocelyn to resolve their problems and to fully explain his rather unusual deli encounters. If, however, Jocelyn intended to persist with her request for a divorce, the letter asserted the allegation should be substantiated as 'Mr Brewer has no knowledge of a person called Sheila Endwhistle.'

* * *

On the same day Bartholomew Bull received Cyril's conciliatory reply, he also received another report from Joshua Shoshowski. It stated that after further investigation he had established that Geoffrey Brewer was not fraternising with a Sheila Endwhistle and that he did not know why Sheila Endwhistle's name had appeared on the anonymous communication. Moreover, he had been unable to obtain any evidence of real acts of adultery. The report concluded that Geoffrey's extramarital adventures were limited to daily bouts of arm wrestling in the New York deli with one Hilda Hessleberg, a wealthy bereaved widow who is a resident of Dorchester Avenue.

Neither Cyril's reply nor Joshua's report received the attention they deserved. Bartholomew Bull was distracted. He had that morning also been handed Cyril's letter on behalf of his wife Pamela by Cindy Bretson. Unknown to the senior partner in Moore Bull & Co, two days had passed since it's receipt in his offices, during which time Cindy had agonised over how to best break the news to him. Having finally despaired over how to categorise the letter and still uncertain about how to handle the grossly unfair and mistaken reference to her in it, she finally decided on simply handing the letter to him and swiftly leaving the room. Confronted by its content, the case of Brewer v Brewer assumed minor significance in Bartholomew's list of priorities. Receipt of Cyril's letter at least clarified for Bartholomew the reason for Pamela's unannounced and mysterious departure from their family home two days earlier for a holiday on her own at an unknown, at least unknown to him, destination.

* * *

Dr Norman Zendlove's unplanned absence from his psychiatric practice for a major hernia operation coincided with Miranda Braithwaite's decision to discontinue analysis. Bi-weekly sessions on the therapist's couch had been replaced by tri-weekly tennis lessons under the personal tutelage of Marius Mountmartin, the Oxton Racquet and Social Club's tennis professional. Marius had achieved local and national fame fifteen years earlier when he had miraculously come through the qualifying rounds at Wimbledon as an unknown, unseeded player to reach the men's singles quarter finals. This career high point resulted in the local council agreeing to the club's request that it grant aid his appointment and annual salary as a professional attached to the local tennis club to encourage the youth of Oxton to achieve international recognition and proficiency.

Now aged thirty-eight, Marius devoted most of his tennis teaching skills to helping the bored housewives of the town's prominent businessmen to efficiently stroke Wilson tennis balls over a tennis court net. In the realm of ball stroking he was king of Oxton and frequently his female clientele's interest in him extended beyond the tennis court to ball stroking of a different type. Bronze with muscular legs and a hint of a French accent inherited from his grandfather, who had wisely settled in Oxton Town shortly before the Second World War broke out and opened a small patisserie, he was regarded by the female members of the club as the most attractive conquest in the town.

By lesson three Miranda had succumbed to his charms and overcome her lifelong antipathy to men whose names commenced with the thirteenth letter of the alphabet. Marius Mountmartin in three tennis lessons proved more successful in helping Miranda overcome her last remaining childhood sexual phobia and inhibition than was Dr Norman Zendlove in sixty-eight sessions of bank-breaking analysis. By the time she reached lesson number ten, Miranda was forced to admit to Marius that like her late father's prematurely deceased secretary, she had become truly hooked by a double 'M' fetish. As far as Marius was concerned it was game set and match.

27

CYRIL BRAITHWAITE was puzzled. In the week following his consultation with Geoffrey Brewer, eight more clients consulted with him after receipt of letters from Moore Bull & Co alleging they were engaged in adulterous affairs. The allegations made were not of themselves unusual. What was unusual was the fact that all of them had received letters in the same week from the same solicitor's firm, signed by the same solicitor, making identical allegations. Even more curiously all eight of them had previously consulted Cyril for bogus reasons soon after he opened for business primarily to get the lowdown on the death of Michael Marshall. Their background details were all stored online in the FILS folder. Moreover, each of them had been persuaded by Ethel to part with a retainer fee of £10,000 prior to their first consultation. Cyril had never previously received £80,000 in retainer fees from new clients in a single week.

All eight of Cyril's new clients informed Cyril that they each had been having a difficult time over the previous couple of weeks with their spouses. None knew why and each denied they were engaged in any adulterous adventures. All eight recipients instructed Cyril to deny they were adulterers, to state their love for their spouses and express themselves surprised by the allegation. As one eloquently put it, 'The Moore Bull letter is a load of bull.'

Cyril, to preserve a modicum of decorum and to avoid further damage to his already frayed relationship with Bartholomew Bull, successfully dissuaded his client from requiring him to so depict the letter in the response he was instructed to send to him.

'Your new client, Lily Podge, has arrived,' announced Ethel sticking her head around Cyril's office door and interrupting his reflections on the oddity of recent events.

'Send her in,' responded Cyril.

A few moments later a well-dressed, obviously slightly nervous woman in her mid-fifties wearing a smart light blue jacket and slacks walked through the open door and was greeted by Cyril with a handshake and directed by him to sit by the coffee table. Having fetched his notebook from his desk Cyril joined her.

'Now before we start, Mr Braithwaite you should know that I am consulting with you about a family problem and my husband is Judge Gerard Podge, who presides over Oxton's divorce county court,' said Lily Podge. 'I think you have appeared before his court so I need to check whether you can represent and advise me.'

'I can think of no reason why I can't. Yes, I have represented clients in divorce cases before him but we are not friends nor have we ever socialised together,' Cyril replied.

'Ok that's a relief. This is just an exploratory meeting. We have been married for over twenty-five years and I still love my husband, but things have got really strange over the last two years. As well as taking me through my legal rights and wrongs I'm hoping you might be able to suggest how to solve my problem. I reckoned after you experienced the unconventional death of Michael Marshall there's not much that would shock you and you're really the only solicitor I feel comfortable discussing this with. But first I need your assurance of absolute confidentiality. I don't want any of your staff to know the details nor do I want you to maintain any record of what I tell you other than to record I consulted with you about a family problem. I don't think you are going to forgot what I am about to say.'

Intrigued by his new client's unusually coherent introductory comments, Cyril instantly agreed and gave the confidentiality assurance sought. Having obtained from Lily Podge a straightforward background history of her marriage, her work as a public relations consultant, the family's property ownership and income and learnt that their two, now adult children were both university students who no longer lived at home, Cyril asked Lily to explain the reason for their meeting.

'Well Mr Braithwaite, it's simple but weird. As you may know Gerard has been adjudicating on divorce and family cases for over five years now. He has led a fairly good and sheltered life and we have had throughout our marriage a great relationship. He is a very conventional guy, or at least was. I think some of the cases he has dealt with have had a strange impact on his psyche and how he sees the world... er... his world. His behaviour has dramatically changed and I don't think I can cope anymore.'

Dying with curiosity, Cyril asked the blindingly obvious. 'In what way has it changed?'

'During the day he is fine. He has his breakfast, heads off to court, does his thing as a judge, most times when he comes home goes out for a light jog or a walk. Then he showers, we have our evening meal and we chat, watch television or read. Sometimes we discuss cases that came before his court. Occasionally, on an evening he disappears into his study to research some legal point relevant to a case he is hearing. It is all so normal up to that point. It is when we are about to retire to bed that the trouble starts.'

Unsure of where the conversation was going, Cyril anticipated some talk of violence, rubber dolls, handcuffs or viewing online porn on xHamster or Pornhub. He did not anticipate the judicial journey into a regressive personality disorder and delusions of infancy about to be revealed.

Lily Podge hesitated and there was a brief silence broken by Cyril.

'And what is the nature of the trouble you mentioned?'

'He doesn't wear pyjamas going to bed. He wears one of a selection of blue or green adult size babygros or what you might call a baby's onesie or a baby sleep suit. They are large replicas of what babies wear that he purchases from some idiosyncratic online website. They are all decorated with images of bright yellow teddy bears. Before dressing in a babygro he insists I help him put on a large adult-sized nappy. It is very disturbing but I can't get him to properly discuss or explain it. I have done some of my own research and it seems that he has a condition or disorder called paraphilic infantilism and is acting out some form of age regression. When dressed in the babygro he starts babbling like a baby and demands his bottle. I have to fill an oversized baby bottle he purchased from the same website with warm milk. He even insists that I hold the bloody thing while he drinks from it.'

'I see,' responded Cyril who didn't really and was struggling not to laugh as he conjured up an image of Judge Gerard Podge sitting in court wearing a babygro and hearing a case as he sucks on the teat at the end of a baby bottle. 'I can understand you find that troubling. Why does he wear a nappy? Does he have an incontinence problem?'

'The nappies are marketed for the adult incontinent. Thank god that is not an additional problem. If it were he would probably demand I change his bloody nappy. The only incontinence Gerard displays is of the verbal variety when he gets worked up about something that annoys him. But no. He has no problem of that nature. He just regresses to baby mode and throws an occasional tantrum. It's like dealing with a two-year-old in a man's body,' explained Lily. 'I think it's some type of defence mechanism to return to a happier time to protect himself from the stress and trauma caused by what he hears in court.'

'And you have tried to discuss what he is doing with him?' asked Cyril, struggling to retain a sympathetic expression of serious concern.

'Yes but it's useless. All he says is that it's some sort of compulsion. After being fed his bottle he then sleeps like a baby for eight hours. On occasions when I have said no to bottle feeding he has burst into tears and thrown a tantrum. Have you ever seen a man in his mid-fifties dressed in a babygro throwing a tantrum, Mr Braithwaite? It's terrible. So upsetting. I've learnt the simplest thing is to give in and role play with him. One of the worst parts is when he calls me mother. I'm not his bloody mother. I'm his wife,' asserted Lily, her composure totally disintegrating as she fought back tears.

Saying 'take your time', Cyril allowed a couple of minutes of silence to elapse as Lily wiped her eyes with a small handkerchief and regained her composure.

'What happens in the morning when Gerard wakes up?' he asked.

'He leaves the bed, cleans his teeth and washes his face and gets naked in the bathroom. He then strolls back into our bedroom, acting normally as if nothing is wrong and gets dressed. During the week it's shirt, suit and tie. At weekends, casual wear. Nothing remarkable or unusual. It is as if the night before never happened and it isn't a topic he is willing to discuss. It's all very bizarre. For the sake of a quiet life I let the day roll on but I can't take it any more, Mr Braithwaite. Something must be done.'

'What is it you would like done?' queried Cyril.

'I want him to stop it, to return to normal. We had twenty-three happy years before all of this started. Basically, I want to return to normal, not travel down the divorce route. Do you, Mr Braithwaite, have any suggestions?'

'Would he or both of you engage with a psychiatrist or family counsellor to try and work through this?' Cyril asked.

'So far he has rejected that idea but maybe a letter from you asking that he does and explaining that if he refuses to co-operate I might have to seek a divorce will bring him to his senses and produce something positive. What do you think?'

'Can't do any harm,' Cyril replied. 'Let me prepare a draft letter for you to approve and we can see what happens.'

'I haven't mentioned his incessant playing of the Baby Shark song and his early every Sunday morning watching Peppa Pig cartoons at a time when in the past he used to watch the Andrew Marr programme on BBC One which, of course, is now no more. I've tried to get him to watch Laura Kuenssberg, who's taken over from Marr, but he says she isn't as entertaining as Marr. I can't stand Peppa Pig or that bloody song. 'S'pose no purpose in mentioning that in your letter?' Lily wondered.

'I think you've got more serious troubles than either of those. Likely both come with the territory,' said Cyril.

After Cyril had explained the complexities of divorce law and Lily's entitlements should things not work out, the consultation ended. Cyril instantly sat down to personally draft and type the letter he agreed to prepare, personally post to Lily for her approval and keep a copy hidden in his office safe. As he did, so the lyrics and music of Baby Shark, Pinkfong's infuriatingly catchy children's song, repetitively played in his head.

28

AFTER OFFICE HOURS the Oxton Racquet and Social Club was the focal point of Ethel Edelwitz's outside office activity. On Monday and Thursday evenings she participated in aerobics; Wednesday evenings, social tennis; on either a Saturday or Sunday throughout the year, weather permitting, Ethel played in the club's mixed doubles tennis tournaments and on most Friday evenings in the club bingo session. There was also the occasional club barbecue and Saturday night dinner that she enjoyed.

Ethel took her aerobics particularly seriously. She loved swinging her arms, legs and hips in rhythmic co-ordination to the repetitive invigorating beat of Caribbean music under the watchful eye and tutelage of Charmaine Beechcroft, the St Lucian wife of Douglas Beechcroft, the manager of the Oxton branch of the Midland Bank.

Douglas was regarded locally as a reticent, financially cautious man of conservative taste in all things. It was Douglas who was responsible for the registered letter received by Cyril about the dire state of his bank account after Michael Marshall's death and his ceasing to work in his late father-in-law's law firm. Unknown to the local towns folk the Douglas Beechcroft they knew utterly changed character when on Christmas and summer holidays he flew off to the Caribbean islands in search of sun, sex and excitement.

When in the Caribbean, Douglas's familiar pin stripe suits, immaculately laundered white shirts and sombre dark blue and dark red ties were abandoned and replaced by bright yellow or pink shorts accompanied by loud red, yellow or lime green tops and multi coloured bandanas. The straight backed, strutting, military-style march seen daily as he entered and exited the automated security doors of Oxton's lone branch of the Midland Bank was replaced by a hip swinging, shoulder flopping, gyrating gait of surprising seductive rhythmic complexity and grace. It was during one of his three week fully inclusive summer holiday visits to Club International St Lucia that he fell head over heels in love with Charmaine Lloyd, the daughter of a local lobster fisherman and the resort's deputy manager.

Charmaine was employed as the resort's head aerobics instructor, who 7.30 a.m. every day on a loudspeaker, amplified throughout the resort's grounds, loudly ordered into aerobics action on the beach her wide eyed, pot smoking, alcoholically hung over, semi-comatose early morning volunteers. The decibel level of her larynx would have guaranteed her graduation from any British army officers' military academy with full honours and the highest commendation. It was not only her finely tuned aerobically sculptured body and beauty but also her clearly articulated authoritative commands that turned Douglas on the very first morning he staggered out of bed to join her beach side aerobics class. His admiration for her grew as the days wore on, his fitness improved and his body's flexibility increased. By the end of week two Douglas confessed to an initially sceptical and unimpressed Charmaine that she was the woman of his dreams and begged her to return to England with him as his wife. Initially rejecting his advances, she assumed he was yet another lonely male vacationer in search of an easy entertaining fuck. After much pleading and considerable deliberation, which included, at Douglas's instigation, her carefully examining online the current balance in his Midland Bank deposit account and his pictures of Oxton Manor House, Charmaine succumbed to his marital embrace. Upon her doing so Douglas gave silent thanks to his recently deceased mother, Betty, from whom he had inherited both the monies and house as her only child. Her exquisite timing in departing this world six months earlier and turning him into a man of real means he understood was the closest he would ever come to winning the lottery.

A day prior to Douglas's scheduled airline departure from St Lucia the betrothed couple celebrated their wedding in the resorts simple open roofed wooden wedding parlour erected on a hill overlooking a beautiful sandy beach. Douglas purchased a pair of purple and yellow shorts specially for the occasion, which were accompanied by a new yellow top with a startlingly large picture of a demented parrot. Charmaine wore, at her mother's insistence, her mother's white wedding dress, which had been carefully stored in plastic for twenty-eight years and smelt of moth balls. Their exchange of vows just after the sun set was followed by wild applause from forty-two fully dressed members of staff and twenty hotel guests invited to attend, all in swimwear, except for one who had his tackle fully on display having directly joined them from the resort's small naturist beach. For a reason understood neither by Douglas nor Charmaine, immediately after the applause stopped the five-man resident resort band commenced an incongruous musical rendition, calypso style, of Chris de Burgh's 'Lady in Red'. As everyone started to dance to the peculiar rhythm and Douglas stared lovingly into Charmaine's eyes, Charmaine thought lovingly about the large sum in Douglas's bank account and his pictures of Oxton Manor House. For each of them it was an unforgettable moment of true romance.

Their wedding ceremony was a last-minute insertion into the resort's long planned wedding schedule by Charmaine's mother, Veronica, exerting her authority as deputy resort manager. Due to a behind the scenes row that occurred their ceremony was then somewhat delayed, but neither Douglas nor Charmaine complained, nor did it occur to anyone that the delay could create a problem. Fortuitously, as it may have spoilt their day, neither Douglas nor Charmaine were aware of the angst their unscheduled and unplanned ceremony caused three other couples who had their nuptials unexpectedly delayed, despite months earlier booking a three couple wedding to take place just as the sun was setting in the background. Each bride had especially worn red wedding dresses to match the red shimmering glow of the distant sea as the sun disappeared over the horizon before night fell. When co-ordinating their simultaneous marriages to take place on the resort's beach all three couples believed themselves to have planned something truly romantically unique, lacking all knowledge of the number of couples daily dispatched through the treadmill of the commercially lucrative St Lucian marriage market the resort beneficially exploited. Had the couples realised the weddings would not take place until darkness fell and would be by candlelight each of the brides made it clear to the resort management, that is to Charmaine's mother, Veronica, that they would have worn white and not asked for 'Lady in Red' as their ceremonial musical grand finale. Had they realised that, under St Lucian law any open-air marriage solemnised after sunset was invalid, they likely wouldn't have bothered getting married that day at all and demanded a refund on the entire cost of their much-anticipated romantic vacation.

Utilising her ten years of experience as deputy resort manager and anxious to restore peace and harmony after the unscheduled row, Veronica had successfully urged all three couples 'to stay cool and enjoy the occasion', enigmatically saying 'stuff happens'. As the 'stuff' had already happened there was in practical terms little the couples could do other than get on with their pre-arranged group nuptials and knuckle down and enjoy the alcohol fuelled celebration that followed. Charmaine's mother contributed to their good cheer by announcing there would be no additional charge for the fresh lobster supplied by her husband and the gigantic thickly iced triple decker wedding cake specially ordered.

Charmaine's surprise arrival in Oxton as Douglas's bride was a focus of gossip for many months – discussion primarily focusing on what a beautiful women twenty years his junior saw in Douglas other than a large bank balance and an oversized somewhat dilapidated and creepy ancestral home. Unknown to her startled neighbours and the rest of the townsfolk and, even more importantly, unknown to Douglas, Charmaine had some years earlier reached a conclusion about life vaguely similar to the conclusion reached by Cyril Braithwaite when still a second-hand car salesman.

'If you want something in life reach out and go for it mon,' she told anyone interested in his or her future. Compared with Cyril's long-winded and faltering prescription of how to identify and arrive at your lifetime destination when a mere speck of dust travelling through the stratosphere of existence, it was a somewhat more succinct and sophisticated view. As any wise university professor of philosophy might explain it, upon receipt of a suitably comforting and intellectually stimulating stipend rendering it financially worthwhile to consider the issue at all, it was not so much a theory of self-help but a theory that a get up and go for it attitude positively contributes to ultimately achieving a desired objective. In ideological terms Charmaine's philosophy of life was as comparable to Cyril's as Hagel to Marx, Albert Einstein to Boris Johnson or Emanuel Macron to Bart Simpson...

Not one to sit back on her laurels, which were constantly on the move reggae style, six weeks after Oxton Manor became her home, Charmaine secured permission to commence Caribbean-style aerobics classes in the Oxton Racquet and Social Club. The fact that the club had considerable borrowings from the Midland Bank was generally believed to explain the unusually speedy permission secured by her from the club's notoriously languid committee members who rarely took less than six months to deliberate on any proposition relating to possible new club activities and initiatives. Residents of Oxton still laughingly recalled the report, two years earlier, in the Oxton Weekly News of the committee taking over nine months to deliberate on a momentous proposal from the club's bar and restaurant manager that in future cut chives and parsley be incorporated into all egg sandwiches ordered by club members.

Fortunately, for Charmaine and Ethel, who were both partial to chives, the proposal was agreed. Chives in egg sandwiches though, was not their only connection. It was under Charmaine's watchful eye and tutelage that Ethel toned up her muscles and prepared her body for the day when Cyril would finally succumb to her physical as well as her culinary delights and it was the aerobics classes that unexpectedly brought Ethel and Miranda fatefully closer. Had Douglas Beechcroft not taken a summer vacation in St Lucia, the lives of some of Oxton Town's leading residents may have been very different and involved a good deal less excitement and trauma.

29

MIRANDA COINCIDENTALLY joined the Racquet and Social Club shortly after Ethel. Determined to increase her fitness and maintain her slim figure, she became a daily morning aerobics participant and also joined in on most Monday and Thursday evenings. Much to Cyril's relief she ended all interest in tv soaps and reality shows and spent most of her free time working off her excessive energy at the club. Cyril innocently believed that regular tennis matches, coaching and step aerobics was the cause of Miranda's night-time exhaustion. He was entirely unaware of the substantial contribution of Marius Mountmartin to Cyril's quieter, more sedate and less demanding lifestyle.

Miranda carefully concealed from Cyril her intensive, all inclusive, one-on-one tennis tutorials with Marius and remained ignorant of Cyril's secret wish that she fully act out the role of one of her former soap heroes by having a sultry adulterous affair. Her doing so, Cyril reasoned, would facilitate his obtaining a simple and speedy divorce without being left a homeless financial pauper. As a divorcee Cyril was anxious to avoid having to provide Miranda with ongoing, never-ending financial support at the level to which she had become accustomed. He also did not want a forced sale of their Larkspur Grove home, which would result in Miranda retaining most of the proceeds realised due to the money for its acquisition originating from her father. He was anxious to ensure the money from any sale of their home was divided equally between them and that he had sufficient funds to purchase a new home with the help of a modest mortgage.

As far as Cyril was concerned his marriage to Miranda was fundamentally dysfunctional. One evening just prior to his nightly visit to the Ancient Wig and shortly prior to Miranda joining the tennis club Cyril confessed to the rubber tree that he could no longer cope with what he perceived rightly or wrongly as Miranda's outrageous sexual demands. If they continue, he informed the untroubled evergreen, 'I am going to end up as an inpatient in a hospital ward for the sexually traumatised.'

To Cyril, Miranda's night-time sorties and excesses had surpassed any addicted sexual hedonist's wildest fantasies. He required two stiff whiskeys each night to just pluck up sufficient courage to enter their bedroom, not knowing what might hit him or what he might be hit with upon entry. If any of Cyril's clients had been subjected to a quarter of the bedtime assaults of which he was the involuntary victim he would have recommended taking immediate divorce proceedings and guaranteed a successful outcome. Cyril had no doubt that if the ancient matrimonial offence of unnatural practices still existed and could be tried before a jury of twelve men, Miranda would be unanimously found guilty and consigned to a workhouse for life. If she had been one of the wives of Henry VIII, he pleasantly speculated, she would have ended up in the Tower of London and lost her head long ago. For Cyril, what he believed to be a dream wedding had turned into a never-ending personalised nightmare compounded by a linguistically confused Miranda nightly screaming #MeToo,

#MeToo as she slapped his bottom during intercourse and dramatically climaxed, soaking the bed sheets. Should the International Olympics Committee ever designate squirting as a new Olympic sport, Cyril was confidant Miranda would be a leading contender for a gold medal. He gave no thought to whether his nightly bedtime adventures rendered him eligible for any of the newly created Olympic surfing competitions.

Cyril felt trapped in a nightmare of his own making. The last thing he could do was to end his marriage in contested divorce proceedings that would be heard by Judge Gerard Podge in Oxton's divorce county court disclosing even a small proportion of his nightly humiliations. To do so, he believed, would permanently undermine his credibility not only with the court staff and the local judiciary but also with all his legal colleagues and adversaries. Although initially the court documents would be confidential, he knew it was inevitable their contents would become known and would fuel weeks of sordid gossip by the town's legal luminaries over their midday pints or night-time glasses of Pouilly-Fuissé in the Ancient Wig.

Entering their bedroom at night to find Miranda sound asleep, obviously exhausted by her day of tennis and aerobics was for Cyril an unexpected temporary release from what he perceived to be a marital sentence of hard labour for life, accompanied by a judicial exhortation against any remission or early release for good behaviour. Suddenly, his world changed and an unexpected serenity descended over the Braithwaite household. The change was so profound that Cyril found the need to share it with the rubber tree at the end of what he described as week three of his weeks of calm.

'I don't know what has come over her,' he informed the tree in an accidentally knowledgeable comment whilst drinking an after office hours glass of celebratory port of a vintage usually reserved for when a client discharged outstanding legal fees exceeding £10,000.

'The change is so remarkable, it's like living with a different person. An extraordinary metamorphosis. Everything is just so calm and relaxed.'

The rubber tree listened and for once did not nod off. Having seen and heard it all repetitively in Cyril's office it marvelled at his naivety. It had no doubt, having listened to Cyril describe Miranda's past conduct, that she had not simply terminated seeding sessions with Cyril but was seeding elsewhere and likely intending to transplant and dig her roots into someone else. It was all to do with personal growth and the tree understood that Miranda's growth, like its own, was likely stunted by Cyril's presence and lack of imagination. It's genetically coded background, traceable through DNA testing to a distant Amazonian cousin thrice removed, instinctively taught that a tropical storm inevitably follows a period of calm. It reckoned the storm clouds were rapidly gathering, despite Cyril's sunny disposition. Engrossed in the perceptive brilliance of its genetically stimulated reflections, it luxuriated in the deluge of water and bio-feed that Cyril poured into its pot, sinking down to its roots and determined to assert its presence and make its mark.

The next morning when Ethel Edelwitz entered Cyril's office to roll up the blinds and open the windows to let in some fresh air she felt the impact of an eerie green sensation. Every leaf on the rubber tree seemed to have expanded its reach and to be pointing in her direction. She shuddered involuntarily, believing the tree to be watching her every movement. As she rapidly exited, closing the door behind her, she imagined the two new leaves unfurling on the trees top branch to be smiling broadly.

Sitting down behind her desk she resolved to never again eat liver and onions late at night and to stop reading Day of the Triffids, concluding that either or both had clearly had a debilitating impact on her state of mind. She also resolved to buy a pair of decent secateurs. Imagination or not, the bloody rubber tree was taking up too much space in Cyril's office and would have to be pruned.

Just as Ethel was about to write herself a note to ensure she remembered to drop into Oxton Garden Centre to make the necessary purchase the phone rang. Ethel became yet again engrossed talking to another potential divorce client who had been accused of extramarital adventurism. Fortunately, for the rapidly expanding rubber tree the necessity for her to visit the garden centre to purchase secateurs was rapidly forgotten.

30

U NTIL SHE commenced aerobics Miranda had only met
Ethel on three occasions. Firstly, at Michael Marshall's
funeral and secondly, in the offices of Braithwaite Marshall &
Co two weeks after she had been employed by Cyril. Their third
meeting, a much lengthier encounter, took place at a house party
shortly after the first anniversary of the firm's formation. All other
contact between them had been relatively brief and business-like
phone conversations.

Ethel rapidly figured that Miranda's interest in tennis extended
beyond the tennis courts and the luxurious tennis club facilities
and stretched to extra curricular use of one of the club's main
amenities and attractions. Miranda rapidly figured that Ethel's
interest in Cyril extended beyond providing traditional secretarial
and kosher culinary services in the offices of Braithwaite Marshall
and embodied outside office aspirations that so far had remained
unfulfilled.

It wasn't so much what Ethel said about Cyril that resulted
in Miranda's perceptive assessment, but more the glazed look in
Ethel's eyes whenever Cyril's name was mentioned when they
met at aerobic classes or bumped into each other in the tennis
club. In an alcohol-lubricated discussion at the members-only
club Whitsun barbecue, Miranda impetuously told Ethel she was

looking for an easy way out of her marriage to Cyril and Ethel confessed to Miranda that she was looking for an easy way into Cyril. What Cyril actually wanted in all of this was to each of them a small, largely irrelevant detail to be woven into the tapestry of their conspiratorially planned future lives. Unfortunately for Cyril, each of them had without his knowledge become devotees of Cyril's own philosophy of life and they were each determined on its total application in advancing their own personal sense of happiness. They each agreed that in the pursuit of equality a little sociological rebalancing was required and essentially it was time for women to get exactly what they want. If that required some male manipulation it did not matter. They both agreed that men had been dominating and manipulating women for far too long. It was now their turn.

31

JOSHUA SHOSHOWSKI and Bartholomew Bull sat together in the Ancient Wig reviewing the progress made in the cases under investigation following their mutual clients receiving anonymous communications. They now totalled twenty-one. The pattern was consistent. Each had originated with an anonymously authored card containing a warning in re-arranged newsprint about the up to then unknown nefarious secret sexual engagements of their conjugal bedtime partners.

Twenty of the twenty-one were still current and proving to be still a mystery. One case, Brewer v Brewer, had been resolved with a confession by Geoffrey Brewer to engaging in bizarre bouts of deli lunchtime arm wrestling, an acceptance by Jocelyn that he may have had adulterous thoughts but had committed no adulterous acts and with both of them agreeing to six sessions of marriage counselling with the local rector, Peter Howick. It was hoped that counselling would help resolve any remaining 'inter-personal relationship difficulties that could act as a barrier to their enjoying a truly fulfilling marital life together as God intended.' So wrote Cyril in a reconciliation letter designed to restore peace and harmony sent to Bartholomew on Geoffrey's instructions. When sending on a copy of the letter to Jocelyn, anxious to not further rock the marital boat, Bartholomew had resisted all temptation to query the method of communication used by either Cyril or Geoffrey to ascertain God's intentions. As far as he was concerned, God, who was not a fee-paying client, had nothing to do with it.

In Brewer v Brewer, as in the other twenty active cases, the identity of the author or authors who levelled the accusations and their purpose still remained a mystery. It was also unclear why in the twenty unresolved cases the allegations were general and not specific. The name of no sexually engaged third party had been disclosed while in the Brewer case Sheila Endwhistle had been mistakenly identified as the accomplice to adultery. Joshua conveniently failed to inform Bartholomew that the maligning of Sheila had resulted in his uncovering an unexpected rich vein of knowledge about the local constabulary that might prove useful to him at some future date.

'I have followed all twenty alleged adulterers on various occasions but I have seen nothing to suggest any of them are getting up to no good, sexually speaking, behind anyone's back. A couple have fairly questionable business acquaintances but nothing more. You have received denial letters written by Cyril Braithwaite on behalf of each of them and there is no evidence that they are lying. In order to preserve confidentiality, each of your clients believe their case to be unique and neither the recipients of the accusatory cards nor, presumably, the accused Cyril represents know of identical accusations and denials affecting others,' Joshua summarised.

'All of your clients are now experiencing some marital problems due to the suspicion and mutual antagonism sown. The numbers involved make it inevitable in a small town like

Oxton that at least a couple of them will at some stage disclose to each other their mutual predicament, realise the peculiarity of each being wrongly accused of infidelity and create a further layer of complexity. It seems to me the one thing they all have in common is that you represent twenty people who have received anonymous messages and Cyril represents twenty people who deny anonymous allegations made against them. You and Cyril are the common denominator. I know you and Cyril are well known for practising family law but you would expect that some other solicitors would represent at least a few of the estranged,' concluded Joshua as he lowered his pint of ale.

Up until that moment it hadn't occurred to Bartholomew that there was something distinctly odd about he and Cyril being on opposite sides in so many family breakdown cases that had with unusual rapidity successively appeared over the legal horizon. He had to acknowledge Joshua was on to something. What the something was, however, remained a mystery. In the context of how the various allegations originated it was all decidedly odd.

As unexpected as a thunderbolt followed by a monsoon-like downpour flooding the entire Sahara Desert, the senior surviving partner in the town's oldest law firm in a moment of legal clarity and insight of scholastic proportions suddenly recalled there was another active divorce file which fell into the Bull v Braithwaite legal conflict classification – his own. Until that moment he had failed to suspect that there could be any connection between the Oxton Twenty and himself. Other than he and Cindy Bretson no one in his firm knew he was a potential personal litigant motoring along the road of marital disharmony. He had kept it quiet from his partner Jonathan Moore as he did not want him to freak out at the possibility of yet another firm scandal involving a partner and a secretary going sexually rogue, and Cindy Bretson had been willingly sworn to secrecy.

It was a week since his receipt of Cyril Braithwaite's letter and he had still not replied. Before doing so he wanted to first talk to Pamela to discover what the hell was going on. So far he had been unable to contact her, she was not responding to his phone messages or texts and she was still abroad at some unknown destination. The only communication he had received from her was a cryptic text received a day after her departure saying she required time 'to think about things' and 'in order to stimulate her thinking' she had 'decided to take in a little sun, sea and sangria'.

Bartholomew wondered whether Pamela was also a target of the town's anonymous correspondent. It seemed likely. He could not fathom why she had consulted with Cyril Braithwaite and then taken off without talking to him first. He realised that to assist his investigation he had better disclose to Joshua his own puzzling bit of domestic difficulty as it seemed likely both he and Pamela were caught up in the same web of intrigue as his twenty clients.

All of these illuminating thoughts formed a part of Bartholomew's stream of consciousness as Joshua Shoshowski sat opposite him in the Ancient Wig quietly concentrating on lowering another pint as he awaited Bartholomew's new instructions. He had done his bit as far as he was concerned and he reckoned he had fully earned the down payments he had received, even though the originator of all the bother still remained unknown. Joshua felt a strange affection for the mysterious accuser who had considerably boosted Joshua's own personal standing amongst the Oxton legal fraternity and also dramatically improved his economic wellbeing as evidenced by the healthy credit balance in his Midland Bank current account. Joshua had to acknowledge that if it had all occurred as a result of a scam he invented he would have deserved either an Academy Award or a Nobel prize for originality.

32

SATURDAY AGAIN arrived. Cyril, believing Miranda to be playing in a tennis tournament that afternoon, had booked tickets to take Aloysius to a visiting circus performing in Oxton over the weekend. The circus was encamped for two weeks on a local farmer's meadow just outside the town and it was over five years since any such circus visit. Cyril was particularly looking forward to Aloysius's reaction to his first live performance by circus clowns.

As Cyril and Aloysius sat down just before the show began two familiar figures hurriedly entered the offices of Braithwaite Marshall & Co and accessed the FILS folder on Cyril's laptop. They then addressed a series of envelopes, enclosed messages, sealed the envelopes, put on postage stamps, shut down the laptop they had accessed and departed, taking the envelopes with them.

Watching the unexpected Saturday afternoon activity the rubber tree stood silent guard in the corner of Cyril's office. Although it had no idea what was going on it welcomed the silent monotony of a Saturday afternoon yet again being interrupted by some brief unexpected company. While it appreciated its temporary companions brightening up its day by putting on the lights, it longed for the blinds to be opened and for the sun to touch its outstretched leaves. A gust of wind through an open window would have been regarded by it as an added bonus. However, the blinds remained down and the windows firmly shut. The watchful evergreen realised that its familiar visitors were anxious to ensure that their presence went unnoticed by any passer-by and wondered why.

An hour after they had arrived at the offices the visitors departed. The building was again plunged into darkness and the rubber tree was left alone with its vegetating small companion. Unknown to its temporary visitors, their arrival and then departure from Cyril's office was observed by Joshua Shoshowski who, on a mission of his own, coincidentally saw them entering the office when driving past. Out of curiosity he stopped and parked his car twenty yards up the road, hung in observing Cyril's office until its visitors departed and took their photographs. 'Now there's a thing,' he eloquently muttered to himself as he drove off after their departure. 'There really is a thing! Who would ever have guessed?'

33

DOUGLAS AND Charmaine Beechcroft each sat stunned in Cyril's office. They wished to make their wills and to arrange to place the Manor House in their joint names. Douglas was conscious that being much older than Charmaine, he was likely to go first and wanted to ensure Charmaine was fully protected. Charmaine was conscious that Douglas being much older than her, he was likely to go first and wanted to ensure that both the house and her finances were secured. In short, she wanted to implement their St Lucian prenuptial oral agreement without delay.

Everything had been going well until Douglas, after giving Cyril a copy of their marriage certificate, cheerily mentioned the delay to the start of their St Lucian wedding ceremony, resulting in their not exchanging vows until after sunset.

'Are you sure of that?' Cyril had asked.

'Sure of what?' asked Douglas.

'That you did not exchange your vows and that you were not pronounced man and wife until after sunset?'

'Totally certain,' replied Douglas. 'It was really romantic. We both said "I do" with candlelight in the background. But why does that matter?'

'Well transferring a house from a husband's sole name into

the joint names of a husband and wife generates minimal expense and has no major tax implications. The opposite is the case where a couple have resided together for just a short time and are unmarried. Similarly, if Charmaine was to inherit your assets and funds as your wife she would pay no inheritance tax, but if she did so as a stranger there would be considerable tax payable.'

'Well that's all right then, as we are married,' responded Douglas.

'Well that's the problem,' said Cyril. 'Under St Lucian law your marriage outdoors by the beach is invalid once solemnised after sunset. If invalid in St Lucia, it is also invalid in England.'

'Are you saying that according to English law we are not a married couple?' asked Charmaine. 'Does our wedding certificate not matter?'

'That's what I'm saying,' replied Cyril.

'So at the moment we are living in sin,' asserted Charmaine.

'Well, if it comes to religion, you are living in sin whether or not your St Lucian wedding is valid. Am I not right in understanding it was a civil not a religious ceremony? On that basis it is not recognised by any church. But it is civil not religious recognition that you require for legal purposes.'

'Oh dear lord. This is all too much. I don't want to live in sin.'

'Well you are not really,' interrupted Douglas. 'You are living in Oxton Manor House in Herbitshire in King Charles' England.'

'Not bloody funny, Douglas, and stop smiling.'

'Well I'm smiling cos this, I think, is easily rectified. We can again marry, this time in Oxton, and problem solved. Am I not right, Cyril?' Douglas asked.

'That's it,' replied Cyril. 'And to avoid sin we can ask the rector to solemnise the marriage, so it will be both a civil and religious ceremony all in one.'

'Even better, we can have my mother at it,' exclaimed Douglas.

'But she is dead, how can she be at our wedding?' asked Charmaine, startled.

'Don't get that,' announced Cyril.

'Well leave it to me,' said Douglas. 'I'll talk to Rector Peter Howick and it will be all arranged. Cyril, you will join us and act as a witness won't you?' Douglas asked.

Intrigued and anxious to retain Douglas's legal business Cyril quickly agreed. He was used to arranging the termination of dead marriages. He was now apparently to attend a marriage in the presence of a dead mother-in-law. For that there was no known law at all. Life in Oxton just kept on getting weirder and weirder, insofar as that was possible.

* * *

Sheila Endwhistle was determined to end her marriage and to shack up with Chief Superintendent Charles Morrow. She wanted more to life than just occasional interludes of delicious sex in Oxton Woods interrupting a lifetime of marital disharmony and flatulence with Fred. She decided it was time for a new initiative. She discharged the long outstanding fees she owed to Cyril Braithwaite, which had remained unpaid for over a year and a half despite several reminders and ultimately letters threatening to sue authored by Ethel. A week later she phoned to make an appointment.

'Hello, Braithwaite Marshall & Co,' said Ethel answering the phone.

'Oh, hello, this is Sheila Endwhistle,' said the caller breezily.

'I'd like to arrange an appointment to talk to Mr Braithwaite.'

'Oh that is really interesting. How about 3.30 p.m. the second Tuesday in April in two years' time?'

'Tuesday the, er, what date at 3.30?' queried Sheila uncertainly.

'In April two years away,' responded Ethel sarcastically. 'Isn't that about the length of time you take to pay for his services?'

'Oh that, er, slight delay, er, in paying the bill. I am really sorry, it was something of an oversight,' confessed Sheila.

'Do you need to have your eyes tested then?' queried Cyril's plain-speaking woman Friday. 'No response to fifteen reminders is something more than an oversight. Blindness upon receipt of a lawyer's invoice is new to me. Maybe you need an optician not a solicitor. Mr Braithwaite is far too busy to meet clients who don't pay their bills. I assume if you didn't again require his help, you would still be optically incapacitated and we wouldn't have finally received your cheque in the post three days ago.'

'Well if that's your attitude I'll go elsewhere,' responded Sheila who decided she would not tolerate her abusive treatment for another second.

Ethel at that moment, having indulged her annoyance, decided to be conciliatory.

'I can arrange an appointment for tomorrow if you first lodge a sum of £400 with me prior to the appointment,' she announced helpfully.

Sheila regarded this proposal as preferable to going elsewhere and having to explain to another lawyer the historical intricacies of her previously failed divorce attempt. The appointment was made and yet again the lives of Sheila Endwhistle, Charles Morrow, Joshua Shoshowski and Cyril Braithwaite were destined to collide.

34

'LET ME SEE, do I have this right. You and the chief superintendent are lovers, want to live together and ultimately marry. Since the divorce case you and Fred are leading separate lives although you have frequently forced him to comply with his marital obligations and you now want to try for another divorce. I have to write to Fred to ask will he agree to a divorce on the basis your home is sold, the monies are divided equally between you both and you are not seeking support or maintenance payments. You realise that if Fred agrees and your new relationship doesn't work out well, you could be in some financial difficulty?' asked Cyril.

'There should be no difficulty, Mr Braithwaite,' interposed the intended fiancé, who had to Cyril's surprise accompanied Sheila to the consultation out of uniform. 'Dolly and I, I mean Sheila and I, intend to marry as soon as possible. But first we have to get Fred out of the way and set up home together,' said Oxton's leading constable, sounding like a Mafia godfather engaged in arranging a contract killing.

'I'm not sure how easy it will be to get him out of the way, er, get his cooperation. You are sure he knows nothing of your relationship?' asked Cyril diplomatically, avoiding any reference to the two neighbours Sheila previously believed Fred knew nothing about.

'We are totally sure,' replied a confident Charles Morrow in reliance on two decades of investigative experience. 'We also both have total faith in your abilities, Mr Braithwaite, having regard to the excellent results you have achieved in court on other occasions when we have crossed swords.'

While Cyril initially appreciated discovering the chief superintendent's faith in his lawyering ability he realised that his unexpected presence in his office was not just to support Sheila and praise him. It was to ensure that Cyril's detailed knowledge of his extra policing activities, learnt during the Joshua Shoshowski prosecution, was not communicated to Sheila. Although as a consequence of her car crash Sheila had some insight into Charles Morrow's hobbies, he had accompanied Sheila to ensure such matters were not unnecessarily dwelt on during the course of that afternoon's conversation.

Consultation over, Cyril saw them both to the door and assured them that he would post a letter to Fred that afternoon. Sitting behind his desk after their departure, recording on his laptop a record of the consultation, Cyril collapsed in laughter, acknowledging that legal practice had its funny side.

'He calls her Dolly, can you really believe that?' he remarked to the rubber tree, which unnoticed by Cyril was unfurling a new leaf in silent celebration of the humorous revelation.

'Dolly,' he laughingly repeated. 'I wonder does he deflate her and stuff her into his briefcase?'

The rubber tree, in an exercise of extraordinary personal restraint, did not respond.

* * *

Joshua Shoshowski parked his car opposite Cyril Braithwaite's office at the very moment Sheila Endwhistle and Chief Superintendent Morrow emerged together into the street and slowly walked to the Jaguar parked about fifty yards down the road. The infatuated pair were a familiar sight to Joshua, having followed them at a respectable distance on at least six occasions on drives deep into Oxton Woods and its environs to discreetly photograph and marvel at their amorous physical contortions within the confines of a Jaguar sports car. Joshua knew that they could have concealed their amorous engagements behind the closed doors of the chief superintendent's home but understood he was anxious to ensure that none of his neighbours could witness Sheila entering it and become potential court witnesses in a second contentious divorce case. The car, however, was not the best location for love making.

The very fact that Sheila could pour herself into Charles Morrow's car was regarded by Joshua as a victory of mind over matter. The fact that the chief superintendent's head had frequently disappeared and remained for some time in between Sheila's outstretched legs and he had continued to breathe oxygen without the assistance of snorkelling equipment was viewed by Joshua as more a victory of matter over mind. For Joshua it was a disturbing cause of cognitive dissonance.

Joshua had watched them both in action the day before from the vantage point of a twenty-five-foot-high oak tree in which he was concealed and had climbed with all the agility of an Oxton Wood squirrel. The chief superintendent's head had been in pole position between Sheila's outstretched legs for about fifteen minutes, his bobbing movements accompanied by much Endwhistle screaming and thrashing about. To Joshua, who gave serious consideration to the possible life-terminating consequences of such sexual adventurism in a confined space, the chief superintendent's unselfish bravery deserved recognition in the King's New Year's Honours List. Clearly, for the two motorised sumo wrestlers, there were more immediately satisfying rewards as Joshua observed from his arbour perch that day through a pair of old horse racing binoculars brought along to ensure he was not reaching over hasty conclusions and confusing a lunchtime woodland's prayer meeting with scenes from Fifty Shades of Grey.

Joshua emitted a sigh of relief upon Charles Morrow's submerged head re-emerging into daylight as he changed position. He then marvelled at the speed with which Sheila whipped off his trousers, cupped his manhood in her outstretched hands and caused a volcanic eruption that if replicated by one of planet earth's still active volcanoes would, by the volume of its emissions, have stalled global warming, possibly ushered in the start of a new ice age and been the cause of a mass extermination.

Ending his irreverent and unremunerative reminiscences as the departing Jaguar sped out of sight, Joshua exited from his more modest vehicle and climbed the stairs into the reception area of Braithwaite Marshall & Co.

'Mr Shoshowski, isn't it?' asked Ethel, instantly recognising the recidivist client who had, after Cyril's final plunge into criminology, burglarised his own lawyer's car. 'You haven't been jailed for more criminality, then?' Ethel queried hopefully.

'Been respectable since Mr Braithwaite's good turn,' came the less than fully frank reply.

'Do you mean his good turn in keeping you out of jail or in

his involuntarily lending you his high-spec car radio and music system?'

'You what?' spluttered Joshua, temporarily lost in linguistic confusion. Having visited Cyril to make a few discreet enquiries and to share his success story as a private eye with his former legal saviour, he now found himself under an unexpected cross-examination by the office receptionist who clearly doubted his newfound respectability.

'The music system you buggered off with outside the law courts is... er, was, Mr Braithwaite's,' Ethel asserted, not feeling any need to deploy diplomatic language to convey her message.

'It was his, was it?' queried Joshua nonplussed.

'It was. Called in to return it have you?'

Just at that moment Cyril appeared at his office door accompanied by a grey-haired elderly woman approximately five foot nine inches in height, dressed in an incongruously bright yellow and pink jacket accompanied by a similar coloured mini skirt that seemed designed to draw maximum attention to her peculiarly protruding varicose veins. She looked to be in her eighties and was walking unsteadily towards the stairs propped up by an impressively thick walking stick specially designed to knock any potential mugger at least temporarily, if not permanently, unconscious.

'You are certain my pussy is properly catered for?' Joshua overheard her remark to Cyril as she slowly descended the stairs.

'The trust fund fully caters for all its needs in the event of your passing away,' Cyril assured her as she disappeared out of sight.

This rather odd exchange afforded Joshua an opportunity to recover from Ethel's verbal onslaught. He decided to try a little humour in his first conversation with Cyril since he unwittingly turned him into the unintended victim of his last act of grand larceny.

'She wants her pussy preserved after she is dead, does she, Mr Braithwaite?' was his opening gambit as his and Cyril's eyes met.

'Her cat, Mr Shoshowski,' came the rapid and clearly unimpressed response from Cyril, immediately recognising the source of the rather juvenile double entendre as the ungrateful lout who had shattered his idealistic illusions about the need for more humanitarian and considerate treatment of the criminal classes. 'She wants her cat cared for after her death, if it's any business of yours. She is a former Bolshoi ballerina,' he added as if that explained everything.

Joshua decided he better try a different tack.

'I've come to pay a debt,' he improvised, rapidly changing the primary purpose of his visit and anxious to bring an end to hostilities.

'What debt is that?' asked an obviously still unimpressed Cyril.

'The money I owe you for the stuff I mistakenly removed from your car after my last court case. I got £1,000 for it and I've come to write you a cheque in that amount.'

'You have, have you? You better come in then,' said Cyril visibly cheering up and ushering Joshua into his office.

Cyril sat down behind the modest desk placed in front of the blocked-up fireplace and gestured to Joshua to sit down opposite him. As Joshua did so he couldn't help but notice that the small rubber plant which had previously rested on the office coffee table in a corner of the room was now sitting in a large pot and had grown so large that it dominated the room. For a moment he wondered was it the rubber tree or Cyril he should be addressing, as undoubtedly the former had a more imposing presence.

'£1,275,' said Cyril anxious to press home his unexpected good fortune.

'What is?' asked a confused Joshua.

'The cost of what you robbed.' replied Cyril.

Joshua without hesitation wrote a cheque for the full amount, anxious to move on to another subject. His embarrassing piece of criminality put to one side, he explained to Cyril the motive for his unfortunate action adjacent to the courthouse and the successful consequences of his unlawful act of self-help.

'As it is now, I am up to my neck in detective work and making a great deal of money. So I want to again thank you for the legal work you did for me, for keeping me out of jail and... er... also for your general contribution to my successfully getting my act together. Another reason for my dropping in relates to a number of cases I have currently on my books. I know it is a bit unethical but can we talk off the record for a few minutes?'

'About what?' Cyril queried warily

'About all the divorce and separation cases involving you and Bartholomew Bull. Do you realise you are now opposite each other in twenty cases, and in all of them your clients are being accused of being unfaithful. Even more unusually, considering the number of people generally engaging in illicit sex or who hate their spouses, all your clients are not only denying the allegations but appear to genuinely want to continue to live with their accusers.'

'I'm not sure we should have this conversation,' said Cyril interrupting Joshua's enthusiastic flow of words. 'Client confidentiality and all that. How do you know about any of this anyway?'

'Because I've been investigating some of the allegations on behalf of Bartholomew Bull's clients,' responded Joshua anxious to establish his credentials and believing he would cause no harm by disclosure of his role.

'You mean you have been spying on my clients, invading their privacy and following them around the place,' retorted Cyril angrily.

'Well, I've been following some of them around but I don't think I have invaded anyone's privacy, Mr Braithwaite. To be quite honest about it, it seems to me they are all squeaky clean and up to nothing,' said Joshua gloomily, anxious to ensure that no further misunderstanding took place between them.

'Then why doesn't Bartholomew Bull say so in his letters to me?' queried Cyril throwing legal caution and concerns about client confidentiality to the wind upon learning information clearly beneficial to his clients.

'Because Bartholomew's clients keep receiving weird anonymous messages alleging various acts of sexual misconduct which result in them insisting that Bartholomew presses on. So far, I have been unable to identify the anonymous correspondent or correspondents. As both you and Bartholomew are on opposite sides not only in relation to the twenty cases, but also in relation to the Bull's own domestic difficulties, I felt it would be helpful if we had an off-the-record chat. The one common thread in all of this is that you are on one side and Bartholomew on the other. Stuck in the middle are all the unfortunate clients and perhaps also Bartholomew's wife, Pamela.'

'I think this discussion may have gone a little bit too far,' said Cyril anxious to have some time to reflect on it all.

'Oh dear, have I said too much?' asked the loquacious son of Maidenhead, not wanting to undermine his status as a private detective 'whose discretion can be relied upon' as advertised weekly in the Oxton Weekly News.

'I just want to think over what you have told me,' Cyril replied reassuringly. 'This is all highly unusual and it may be in the interests of all our clients that Bartholomew and I meet. Did he authorise you to discuss the cases with me?' asked Cyril.

'I suggested to him that I call into your office and he agreed,' replied Joshua being somewhat economical with the truth and realising that in his anxiety to impress Cyril he had gone a good deal further than authorised by his naturally cautious instructing solicitor.

'This is, of course, all off the record. That's agreed isn't it?'

'Yes that's agreed,' replied Cyril rising from his chair and walking towards the door.

'Thanks for the chat and sorry again about your car's music system,' said Joshua, shaking Cyril's hand just before exiting from his office into the firm's reception area.

Joshua temporarily hesitated and took a packet of Wrigley's chewing gum out of his jacket pocket. Mimicking a gesture he had learnt watching a tv detective show, he shrugged his shoulders, unwrapped the gum, stuffed it into his mouth, rolled the wrapping paper and tossed it into a waste paper basket beside Ethel's desk.

'Good throw,' he muttered, staring at the basket and then smiling at Ethel.

'See ya round, pussycat,' he said in his best mimicked New York accent to the scowling face looking back at him.

Having entered on a feline note, Joshua thought it appropriate he exit in the same way. Descending the stairs and walking out into the fresh Oxton air, away from the intimidating presence of the rubber tree in Cyril's office, he started to hum. All worries about him talking too much evaporated. He now knew how the cat felt when served the cream. The presence in Ethel Edelwitz's wastepaper basket of a large amount of obviously cut up newsprint told a story very different to any of those that had originally gone to press in freshly printed pristine copies of the Oxton Weekly News.

35

As was usual in moments of high anxiety or serious deliberation, following Joshua's departure, Cyril conversed with the rubber tree in the hope of gaining some enlightenment.

'An anonymous messenger is not only responsible for the Bull marital disharmony but is also at work in at least twenty other family cases. But who and why?' asked a puzzled Cyril, pouring himself a whiskey. 'Clearly Pamela Bull's suspicions about Bartholomew are without any foundation, as it appears are all the allegations made against twenty of my other clients. It really is all very strange.'

A slight breeze blew through the open office window and the top leaves of the rubber tree appeared to nod in agreement. Like Joshua it had its own suspicion about the identity of at least one obvious culprit but it had no answer to the 'why' question.

Cyril reflected further on the day's unexpected events and, in particular, on the reformed persona of Joshua Shoshowski that had made a surprisingly profitable appearance. The cheque nestling in Cyril's pocket had restored some of his lost faith in humanity and acted as a catalyst to his having a newly acquired uncharacteristically optimistic perspective on the world. It also restored some of his lost faith in his self-help theory of life. Joshua had clearly pulled himself up by his own bootstraps, unfortunately with a little help from a final act of a now redeemed grand larceny from Cyril's car.

'Perhaps I should diversify a bit and again take on some criminal work,' mused Cyril as he reached into his jacket pocket for his £350 gold cross pen to sign the post that Ethel, slipping unobtrusively in and out of his office, had placed on his desk. Five minutes later the post, still unread and unsigned, lay on his desk. Cyril ended searching for his pen. It had clearly departed from the offices of Braithwaite Marshall & Co in the care of someone other than Cyril.

'The bugger's taken it,' Cyril told the rubber tree which had by now lost all interest in the day's happenings and fallen asleep. Dismissing all thought of returning to criminal law, Cyril acknowledged that the world had not changed as dramatically as Joshua's cheque, signed with Cyril's migrating pen, had led him to momentarily believe. However, as the events of the next few days were to prove, Cyril Braithwaite was yet again wrong. For Cyril, if for nobody else, the world was about to change utterly. However, for any outsider looking in and following those events the change would appear quite predictable and not all that dramatic at all.

36

CYRIL BRAITHWAITE sat over a late-night pint in the Ancient Wig pondering the prospect of a meeting with Bartholomew Bull to discuss what he had learnt from Joshua. He decided that first he should talk to Pamela after her return to Oxton from her package holiday in Gran Canaria. He was joined at the table by his sometime protagonist and newly discovered admirer Chief Superintendent Charles Morrow,

'Sheila must be a vast improvement on your previous girlfriend,' Cyril remarked laconically, grinning broadly.

'More stable and less bouncy,' replied Oxton's leading policeman, smiling.

'I've got some good news for you,' said Cyril. 'Fred Endwhistle has not only agreed to a divorce but has offered Sheila £175,000 for her interest in their house. I reckon Sheila's half interest is worth at most £150,000. In return for him paying her £175,000 she is to transfer sole ownership of the home to him and move out within four weeks. He is offering her over the odds as he is anxious to both keep the house and ensure that she doesn't change her mind and stay put. The offer is conditional on all necessary papers confirming agreement being signed within seven days. Sheila will be sent an email tomorrow morning telling her all of this.'

'Well, that's a load off my mind,' responded a clearly grateful chief superintendent.

'Is it to be marriage then?' Cyril cheerfully asked the town's most prominent eligible bachelor.

'Absolutely,' replied the clearly besotted. 'The date, of course, all depends on how quickly you can get the divorce through. We have already agreed that if Fred co-operates Sheila will move in with me. Didn't expect you would be able to sort it all out so quickly. I'm sure Sheila will be delighted.'

It wasn't so much a 'sort out' as a 'surrender', thought Cyril, keeping the thought to himself.

'Well if everything is agreed the divorce should be finalised within three months,' said Cyril. 'I think you can safely plan your wedding on that basis and I expect an invitation to the nuptials. It is always enjoyable to celebrate a wedding instead of managing a break-up.'

'Cyril, you will be the guest of honour. Great job,' responded the ecstatic groom.

It suddenly occurred to Cyril that Charles Morrow might be exactly the right person with whom to discuss the strange goings on in Oxton Town, of which Cyril presumed the local constabulary were blissfully unaware.

'Can I bend your ear confidentially on something that is troubling me?' Cyril tentatively asked.

'Sure, why not?' replied the chief super, perking up at the possibility of giving advice to someone who regularly proffered it to others.

Without revealing the names of any clients or revealing Joshua Shoshowski investigative role, Cyril detailed the epidemic of accusatory cards and correspondence formulated from re-arranged newsprint by an anonymous scribe whose targeted adulterous allegations had caused an unprecedented number of Oxton's inhabitants to seek advice from the town's leading law firms specialising in domestic disputes and family law.

'Motive, the first thing you need to establish is a motive,' Charles Morrow explained. 'Then work back from there and identify the culprit. That's the way I would do it.'

'By looking for a motive you are assuming the person responsible is sane,' remarked Cyril, looking doubtful.

'You are presuming nothing. Even the certifiably insane have motives, albeit crazy. You just try and put yourself in their shoes and ask yourself if you were sending the cards and letters what could you possibly be trying to achieve? Even crazy people do things with some objective in mind, even if it is entirely bonkers. Anyway, your bonkers might be someone else's perfectly normal. It's all a question of perspective,' explained Charles Morrow.

Cyril accepted the bit about perspective. For example, his and Charles' perception of Sheila was entirely different. From Cyril's perspective anyone who wanted to permanently shack up with Sheila must be mad, yet here he was sitting talking to her most ardent admirer who displayed no external symptoms of mental turmoil or decay.

'Ok, let's list all the possible motives,' said Cyril, taking out a pen and a small notebook he kept in his jacket pocket.

'The obvious ones first,' said the chief superintendent, assuming his best detective mode.

'Moral or religious crusade to uphold family values, whatever they are,' said Cyril.

'Revenge,' said Charles.

'Jealousy,' countered Cyril.

'Blackmail,' retorted Charles.

'Incitement to murder,' suggested Cyril.

They both hesitated.

'Well, they are all the classic ones. Let's examine them individually,' suggested Charles.

'You can rule out blackmail. Presumably, if blackmail was the motive the anonymous provocateur would have written to all the alleged adulterers threatening exposure unless they paid up. The beans would not have been first spilled to their spouses or lovers,' said Cyril. 'Now how about jealousy?'

'Couldn't result in so many receiving anonymous messages,' replied Charles

'You are right there. Jealousy or hurt might be the motive for communicating an allegation to one person but not for communicating twenty different allegations to twenty unconnected people,' agreed Cyril. 'Incitement to murder?'

'I don't think so. No one has taken a pot shot at or tried to stick a knife into the back of any of the alleged adulterers,' responded Charles.

'Well, that leaves moral crusade or some sort of revenge obsession,' said Cyril. 'But revenge on who for what?'

'Can't figure that one,' replied Charles. 'Is there anything in any of your client's background which could be relevant? Something you might not have considered when they first sought your help?'

'Not that I know of. The only thing they all seem to have in common is me and Bartholomew Bull as their lawyers,' Cyril replied, recalling Shoshowski's offhand remark. 'In fact, come to think of it, there is one strange aspect to all of this. I seem to be mostly representing those who insist they are wrongly accused, whilst Bartholomew represents most of those who received the anonymous allegations. That's very peculiar. You'd expect a more even divide between the two.'

'Perhaps the author of the allegations recommends Moore Bull & Co as the solicitors to be consulted. Perhaps this has all been conjured up by Bartholomew Bull or someone employed by him to generate business. It is rumoured he has been a little odd since the death of your father-in-law,' said the chief superintendent, wondering was he about to uncover a scandal within the local legal fraternity.

'I'm pretty sure that is not it,' replied Cyril, who had been careful to not mention the added complication of the allegations received by Pamela Bull.

'Looney delusional moral crusader then is the only explanation,' deduced Charles.

'Looks like it,' sighed Cyril, who had briefly hoped the chief superintendent's years of police detection would produce a more earth-shattering explanation.

'But why pick out this particular bunch to target when they all seem to be clean as a whistle as far as sexual malfeasance goes?' asked Cyril. 'From my many other family cases I know there are quite a few people in the town engaged in sexual philandering. For someone who has clearly gone to some trouble it couldn't have been all that difficult to target the truly guilty instead of the generally innocent.'

The chief superintendent shifted uneasily in his seat and remained uncharacteristically silent. Cyril instantly realised his somewhat insensitive and undiplomatic reference to the town's sexual adventurers was a cause of upset in the context of his drinking companion's very personal engagement with Sheila Endwhistle. Continuing their conjecture would, he concluded, result in nothing productive and a change in topic was called for.

'Oxton Rovers going to win again this weekend, you think?' Cyril boldly enquired in the hope of eliciting an animated response from his now silent and sullen drinking companion.

'Dunno,' came the unanimated, disinterested reply.

Another pint was ordered and silence reigned. Both men sat quietly together, introspectively lost in their individual personal confusions. Cyril was sadly conscious that yet again upon his seeking a helping hand none was available to enable him fully unravel the mysterious events in which he and his clients were legally embroiled.

37

BARTHOLOMEW BULL had still not heard from Pamela but as a result of enquiries made to three different travel agents in Oxton Town he discovered she was destined to return from a two-week holiday in Gran Canaria the next day. He was determined to discover exactly why she had got Braithwaite to write to him and why she had flown off to foreign parts with no prior warning. He wondered should he meet her at the airport or wait until she arrived home before they talked. Meeting her at the airport would catch her off guard as he was not supposed to know where she had gone nor the date of her return. Alternatively, it might be better if he waited until she was home as he was unsure of her likely reaction to their meeting and he did not want some embarrassing public scene. Acknowledging to himself that a clear decisive approach was required, he postponed reaching a conclusion on what to do until after his pre-breakfast workout the next morning.

* * *

The text message read, 'Phone me the moment you land. Need to talk to you before you meet Bartholomew. Cyril Braithwaite.'

Cyril knew from previous experience that Pamela frequently ignored for days texts sent to her. After failing to contact her by a follow-up phone call to her mobile a few hours later, he then phoned the hotel and asked the receptionist to arrange for a note to be put under her bedroom door the evening before her scheduled return flight. It simply read, 'Check your texts, Cyril.'

Pamela found the note upon her return to her hotel bedroom late that evening from a Paella Eating Experience recommended by and booked through the hotel concierge as the grand finale of her two-week package holiday. What the concierge failed to disclose was that the paella served on the nearby beach was cooked by his wife and mother-in-law, who had limited culinary skills and who viewed the hotel's tourists as easy targets to exploit. Attacked by intestinal implosions upon entering her bedroom which Pamela reasonably and prophetically feared were the forerunners of a greater drama, she stuffed the note in her handbag and sprinted for the bathroom. The shocking revelations of Bart's philandering had caused the bottom to fall out of her world. Now Pamela discovered it was the world that was about to experience the fall, having accurately anticipated that she and the paella were about to prematurely part company.

Distracted by her digestive trauma and preoccupied by its continuing consequences, it was only the following day when back again in England and disembarking from her plane that Pamela remembered and read the note. She walked into the baggage section of the arrivals hall to await her suitcase's arrival. There was pandemonium as the luggage of the returned packaged travellers speeded past its bemused owners on Conveyor Belt 3 as they pushed past each other, attempting to get into pole position to retrieve it as it hurtled by with unexpected speed, their possessions disappearing down underground tunnelling to again swiftly reappear and hurtle past again.

Pamela's mobile phone had expired on the second day of her holiday. She had absentmindedly forgotten to bring her charger and had decided to not borrow one from the hotel reception, appreciating an opportunity to quietly reflect without being hassled by texts or phone calls from Bart. Ignoring the airport bedlam and temporarily abandoning her suitcase as it rocketed passed like an eccentric missile, Pamela looked around searchingly for an airport phone to make contact with Cyril. As she did so, above the irate grumbling and expletives of the hapless passengers, an incomprehensible airport service announcement attempted to provide some guidance to passengers in search of baggage.

'Glease move ack from convoor belt three as a fau has veloped, the agagge will be traferd to bet two.'

The impact of this unintelligible communication in protecting those around Conveyor Belt 3 from a serious accident and in restoring their faith in the efficiency of airport administration was not immediately evident. Arrival passengers surrounding the renegade belt continued in true kamikaze fashion to lunge and grab at their cases in the largely futile hope of successfully retrieving them. Some of the arrivals were successful. Most were not. One, a frail looking Mrs Janet Arbuckle, eighty-one years of age of diminutive stature, was last seen clinging to a very large and unstoppable Samsonite black suitcase being assaulted by three black rubber flaps singing 'There will always be an England' followed by shouting 'God save the king' as she disappeared from sight into airport oblivion. The shock to the octogenarian of her dramatic exit from the baggage area tragically resulted in her suffering cardiac arrest. Her obituary published in the

Oxton Daily News two days later, recorded Vera Lynn as her favourite singer and Bruce Willis as her favourite movie star. It also disclosed that her favourite film was Die Hard 2, viewed by her twenty-three times many years earlier at the Oxton Savoy cinema. Her surviving husband, Harold, was quoted in a story accompanying the obituary as expressing pride in the courage she had shown when confronted by adversity. As an afterthought he also stated that he expected damages of at least one million pounds from the buggers at the airport who were responsible for her untimely death.

Oblivious to the drama unfolding around Conveyor Belt 3, Pamela finally located an airport phone and called Cyril.

'Braithwaite Marshall & Co,' intoned Ethel.

'Hello, Pamela Bull here.'

'Where's here?' asked Ethel unnecessarily.

'At the airport,' replied Pamela.

'Oh, are you travelling somewhere?'

'No, I've just returned,' Pamela replied despairingly, trying to regain control of the conversation.

'Where were you?' enquired Ethel, as she carefully coated the nail on the little finger of her left hand with Revlon's blush red nail varnish, balancing the phone between her right cheek and her right shoulder.

'In Gran Canaria, if it really matters. Cyril, Cyril Braithwaite, is he there?' shouted Pamela realising her time was about up and she had no more change to feed the phone.

'Yes, do you want to speak to him?' Ethel helpfully asked.

'I do but first can I give you my number? It's, hello, hello... Damn, blast, the bloody phone's gone dead,' Pamela irately announced to the impatiently fidgeting aspirant public phone users who had formed a queue behind her as she talked to Ethel, each anxiously waiting to make contact with the world outside the airport terminal.

'Oh my suitcase. I nearly forgot the bloody thing,' she told no one in particular as she hurried back to the chaotic arrivals baggage area conveyor belts.

The shambles she had temporarily left behind was now replaced by a scene of total bedlam as men, women and children ran between conveyor belts 2 and 3, their Gran Canarian luggage hurtling past grand prix style, at a speed that would have been applauded by spectators at Silverstone Race Track if emulated by formula one racing drivers in the British Grand Prix.

'There is a technical fault on veyer elts two and three,' the helpful super-articulate public announcer told those who hadn't noticed. 'We are sorry for the... convenience caused to assengers. Your agage is very important to us.'

'Not as bloody important as it is to us,' shouted a red faced, clearly sunburnt and agitated male passenger in response.

'We hope the problem will be solbed very soon,' the announcement concluded.

At that very moment the speed at which both belts were travelling dramatically and abruptly increased. Suitcases were propelled into the air temporarily gaining height as impressively as a state-of-the-art Elon Musk spaceship on take-off. They then fell to earth, their neatly packed contents spewing out in every direction. The consequent fallout caused the distraught passengers to scurry frantically for their personal possessions and anyone else's that took their fancy.

Pamela, surveying the scene, stoically regarded it as just another unexpected intrusion into her normally more ordered life. She strode purposefully towards her own battered luggage, indiscriminately kicking the ankles of anyone who got in her way. Stepping forward to reach for her newly purchased lemon-coloured Lacoste tennis top lying on the airport floor her foot landed on something long, hard and vibrating. Temporarily unbalanced, she toppled over and the world turned black. After an ambulance had hurried the unconscious victim of the marauding spontaneously erupting vibrator to Oxton Hospital for a night's observation, airport porters gathered up unclaimed suitcases and their widely dispersed belongings to deposit in the lost property office. Amongst the items found were thirty-three socks (all odd), fifteen bikini bottoms, two bikini tops, seven shirts, three ties, four nappies and thirty-eight vibrating dildos of varied colours, shapes and sizes, a black leather whip and five pairs of handcuffs.

'There were obviously some things no one wished to claim as their own and others just lost or abandoned,' remarked Peter Landing, the airport manager, to his rather dull deputy manager, David Flyer, as he surveyed the diverse collection of battery-operated organs.

'There certainly were, Mr Landing. I couldn't see anyone wanting to be identified with that purple tie with the yellow dots, but I would have expected the police on board to have at least picked up their handcuffs,' the airport's frequent flyer shrewdly replied.

38

BARTHOLOMEW BULL decided the airport's arrivals hall was not the best venue for confronting Pamela about the bizarre allegations contained in the letter he had received from Cyril Braithwaite. He concluded it would be better for her to make her own way home and for him to then instigate a conversation about the letter upon his return from the office that evening. His plan rapidly changed upon being told by Cindy Bretson that Oxton Hospital had phoned to say Pamela had been admitted as a casualty patient, having been taken to the hospital by ambulance from the airport.

Fifteen minutes later Bartholomew was standing at the end of Pamela's bed in the private room allocated to her. She had regained consciousness moments before Bartholomew's arrival and weakly raised her hand to acknowledge his presence. In response, Bartholomew, oblivious to Pamela's pounding headache, instantly launched into a lengthy prepared speech designed to explain the recent confusing events which had led to her becoming an airport casualty. Coming towards its end, he continued, 'So you see, you are not the only one. You and about twenty others have been misled by anonymous communications falsely accusing a variety of people living in Oxton of infidelity. They all contained allegations detailed in newspaper cuttings stuck together from extracts taken, it seems, from the Oxton Weekly News. But the news contained in the messages is fake. None of it is true about any of my clients nor about me. I'm representing most of those who received the fake allegations and Cyril Braithwaite is representing most of the falsely accused. Only he didn't know till yesterday when Joshua Shoshowski met him that anyone other than you had received messages from an anonymous lunatic.'

Pamela lay silent in the bed trying to absorb the crazy story Bart was telling. She wondered was she still unconscious and whether it was all a bad dream or was she awake and hallucinating. She silently took a secret oath to never again eat paella.

'So you see it's all some gigantic hoax. None of it is true. I haven't done anything wrong with Cindy Bretson and none of my clients have done anything wrong with any of the people they have been accused of bonking. It's all nonsense,' Bartholomew emphatically exclaimed, oblivious to the herd of stampeding elephants who at that very moment, uninvited and unprovoked, thundered across Pamela's brow, just below the fourteen stitches required following her impetuously attempting to headbutt the metallic side of Conveyor Belt 2. Fortunately, Pamela was blissfully unaware and happily ignorant of the speculation and gossip caused by her fall and of the legal action in which she was destined to be named as a defendant.

* * *

Jessica Hepworth, sixty-nine years of age, a lifelong resident of Oxton and an arrivals hall returnee from her twenty-ninth holiday in Gran Canaria, adamantly insisted to all she met in the days that followed that the dildo that flew towards her as Pamela hit the ground had originated from under Pamela's skirt prior to crashing into and bruising her right ankle as she unsuccessfully tried to evade its lethal flight. A woman of renowned determination and chairperson of Oxton's local Conservative Association, she had confiscated the offending object immediately after impact. Following her doing so she then announced to anyone willing to listen that it was outrageous that there be any dangerous flying objects in an airport. She also determined to retain the dildo as evidence to use in the compensation claim she intended to bring both against Pamela and the airport authority for suffering not only physical injury but also psychological damage.

'You'd think if she was going to use one of those bloody things she would at least have gone into the ladies first,' Jessica had remarked to a startled luggage porter who, by then, had experienced more airport trauma in half an hour than he or most of his colleagues normally experienced in a lifetime of devotion to baggage handling.

More sympathetic souls concluded that the frustration of airport events had driven Pamela beyond rational thought. They presumed she had deliberately head-butted Conveyor Belt 2 without fully appreciating the likely personal consequences and that she had taken such eccentric action out of frustration upon it becoming clear that simply kicking the side of the conveyor belt together with other disembarked passengers was totally ineffective and did not slow it down. Where the dildo originated from was something of a mystery but the likelihood of it being deployed by Pamela amidst the chaos was deemed minimal.

* * *

Pamela concluded that if the thumping in her head was to ever stop she had to end Bartholomew's incessant ramblings. She also wanted time to ascertain whether he was telling the truth or had concocted some nonsensical fictitious story and was engaged in a bit of self-serving special pleading.

'Look Bart, I don't know who Shoshowski is and I care less. I do know who Cindy Bretson is and I don't like what I think you and she have been doing. I think I understand the gist of what you have been telling me but I want to talk to Cyril Braithwaite before I jump to any conclusions. Now would you ever bugger off and let me sleep,' she delicately concluded, turning on her side and shutting her eyes.

Bartholomew Bull swiftly and silently exited the hospital bedroom. He whistled his way down the main corridor to the front entrance. 'Things are looking up,' he thought. 'Pamela is talking to me again and is almost back to her normal ebullient self.'

He celebrated their resuming communication with a secret bit of self-indulgent biceps and stomach muscle flexing and undulating, concealed, he believed, from public view by the long sleeves of his Charles Tyrwitt pure white cotton stretch shirt. As he drove down Oxton High Street in the direction of his office more than one client of his illustrious law firm quickly concluded should they in the future have any legal difficulties they should seek legal help elsewhere. The strange muscle spasms causing Bartholomew to jerk up and down in his car as he drove along and waited at traffic stops confirmed to those who noticed that there really was some truth in the spreading rumour of the serious deterioration taking place in the physical and mental health of the senior partner of the town's oldest legal practice. At the very least he presented as suffering from an extreme version of Tourette syndrome. From the shirt manufacturer's perspective, had they known of Bartholomew's unconventional car exercising, there is little doubt that they would have approved of his publicly demonstrating and validating the stretching capacity of their shirts acclaimed fabric.

39

IT WAS THE START OF a new week. Upon Cyril arriving at his law firm he unexpectedly discovered sitting in his waiting room one of the clowns who he and Aloysius had seen perform in the circus the previous weekend. Recognition was instant as his face was painted white, he had a large bulbous red nose, outsize matching red eyebrows and wore a multicoloured large shirt with matching large pyjama pants. The pants appeared held up by red braces. A yellow cap with an oversized purple peak and small pink stars sat on the chair beside him. Cyril recognised the cap. Muttering, 'Be with you shortly,' he hurried into his office, lifted the phone and asked Ethel to join him.

Ethel explained that a short time earlier the clown, who said he was called Charlie Chuckles, had called in and sought an urgent meeting with Cyril. She had received an early morning notification that Cyril's court case scheduled for that day was postponed due to the judge falling ill over the weekend. As he had no appointments in his diary, she had told Mr Chuckles to await Cyril's arrival. She had also informed the client by phone of the postponement of his case to another date and opened and sorted that day's post.

'Shall I direct Mr Chuckles in to you?' she asked Cyril.

'Why not, he might be good for a laugh. Aren't you taking the day off?' enquired Cyril.

'Yes, will be gone in a few minutes. Have lots to do at home. Just wanted to get the post open, run off any important new emails and ensure your day was organised. With the court case postponed why don't you take some time out also?' asked Ethel.

'Now there's a good idea. Maybe a couple of drinks in the Ancient Wig and then an afternoon walk in Oxton Woods.'

'Go for it,' enthused Ethel. 'I'll send in the clown.'

Looking the epitome of misery, the clown shuffled, head down, into Cyril's office and sat slumped in the chair proffered by Cyril beside his coffee table. Cyril sat down opposite, notepad and pen in hand.

'Thank you for seeing me at such short notice, Mr Braithwaite. The circus gets back on the road and is leaving Oxton in a couple of days. I recognised you in the audience last weekend from your newspaper photos and thought you the right man to talk to for advice and help.'

'Well first let me check out one thing. Is your name really Charlie Chuckles?'

'No, that's just my artistic name, even though everybody, including my wife, calls me Charlie. My real name is Alphonse Smiley.'

'Well I can understand you dropping the Alphonse, but why drop the Smiley?' asked Cyril, curiosity getting the better of him. 'Would Smiley not have worked well for a clown?'

'Well at one stage I was known as Wiley Smiley but I changed it. The circus manager said that name didn't induce audience laughter and just upset people who had clown phobias and were afraid of clowns.'

Cyril, regretting he had asked, decided to be more directional.

'Ok, I understand. So what brings you here so early in the day?'

'Coulrophilia and I can't take it anymore.'

'What on earth is coulrophilia?' asked Cyril, looking puzzled.

'A sexual attraction to clowns. My wife will only be intimate and have sex if I am dressed like this. It is some sort of kinky obsession with clowns. I am also hit on at shows and stalked by women in the audience turned on by clowns. The ones over seventy also frequently try and grab my testicles. I just can't take it anymore.'

'Well, what is it you would like me to do? Have you considered another profession?'

'I am trying to work that out. I have worked as a clown for almost fifteen years. Apart from audience harassment I just can't cope with people laughing at me anymore. I am a serious person and want to be taken seriously.'

'Well as a lawyer I don't think that is something I can fix.'

'If I quit work can you sue the circus for me, so I leave with some money?'

'Sue them for what?'

'Well firstly for sexual harassment, audience ball grabbing. Secondly, I've read a lot about post-traumatic stress disorder. I am constantly wired and unable to sleep. When I do sleep, I have crazy dreams and nightmares. I think I must have PTSD. Can't the circus be sued for making me work in a stressful environment? The more miserable I am and look when in the circus ring, the more the audience laughs. It's intolerable but the management insists I perform and work through my contract.'

'Well employers are supposed to ensure employees have a safe working environment but I don't think requiring a clown to work in a circus ring where he gets laughed at in any way breaks the law,' explained Cyril, trying not to laugh. 'You are expected to generate laughter. That's the job.'

'Thought in this day and age there would be some legal protection for clowns. After all we are an endangered readily identifiable minority. As a member of that minority, I am being demeaned, harassed and discriminated against. It really is a rotten world,' Charlie despairingly asserted.

'Have you informed the circus manager of the sexual harassment?'

'I have but he thinks I am joking. He says no one falls for clowns and just laughs.'

'Well, there may be something in that but not much,' said Cyril.

'And what about my wife? She insists I permanently dress as a clown, even at night in bed. She says it turns her on and stimulates her having sexual fantasies. Whenever we make love she constantly laughs, sometimes hysterically. It is in the midst of hysterical laughter when she usually has an orgasm. She also makes me throw custard pies in her face and hold balloons between my teeth. It is totally demeaning, demoralising and contributing to my PTSD. I don't want to be laughed at when making love. I don't want to throw bloody pies at her. I don't want at the age of thirty-seven to have to take Viagra every time so that her laughter doesn't undermine my capacity to sustain an erection. She has totally undermined my self-confidence and my remaining self-esteem. If I ditch the clown outfit when not performing in the circus and refuse to wear it in bed at night, will you please, Mr Braithwaite, represent me in any divorce proceedings she takes?'

Cyril thought he had heard about every possible variety of marital disharmony. He now realised that there is always going to be something new that crosses his desk. The possibilities are endless. He could understand his client not wanting to be laughed at by his wife when being sexually intimate but could not fathom a clown suffering from PTSD due to being laughed at by a circus audience. Suddenly Cyril remembered an advert he had read in the Oxton Weekly News in which Johnny Bleak, the manager of Oxton Town Cemetery, sought applications for the job of assistant cemetery manager. Cyril knew Johnny was due to retire in a year's time and wanted to train in a potential successor.

'I take it that if you stop work as a clown you will want some job which doesn't result in people laughing at you,' said Cyril.

'That's it,' replied Charlie, 'but I have yet to identify what to work at and I have no college degree or special skills outside clowning.'

'Well, there is a job available in Oxton that might fit the bill, and if you are interested, I could put in a good word. I'm owed a favour for recently helping to discreetly resolve what could have been an unpleasant controversy.'

Five minutes later yet another stress-reduced satisfied client left Cyril's office. Cyril had successfully arranged a job interview for Charlie with Johnny Bleak for a position which rarely generated any laughter. Cyril agreeing to represent him should his wife issue divorce proceedings also caused Charlie to smile as he walked up the high street to hail a taxi back to the circus. Unnoticed by Charlie, an elderly woman he walked passed, who suffered from a fear of clowns, fainted on the pavement at what she perceived as a sinister expression on the face of a clown she did not expect to spot on Oxton's high street at eleven o'clock in the morning. The circus manager's judgement that no one falls for clowns was irrefutably disproved.

Cyril turned on the office radio and reflected on yet another job well done as he made himself a morning cuppa. Fortunately, he did not know that his newest client's PTSD and wish for quiet intimacy devoid of laughter was the root cause of repetitive dreams in which he was arrested by police in a cemetery for engaging in necrophilia. Cyril sat contentedly at his desk drinking his morning coffee and reading that Monday's Guardian. Engrossed in the newspaper, he was entirely oblivious to the background sound of Barbra Streisand singing ' Send in the Clowns'.

40

THEY GATHERED IN the small church adjacent to the entrance to Oxton Cemetery. Rector Peter Howick stood at the front of the church on a slightly raised platform. Charmaine and Douglas stood in front of him looking up. Cyril sat in the front row beside the cemetery manager, Johnny Bleak, who had an hour earlier completed interviewing Charlie Chuckles. The aspirant assistant manager, dressed as a clown, sat beside his hoped-for future boss.

There was only one aisle of seating and the rest of the congregation sat in rows behind them. Douglas had invited all the town notables and all those who worked with Charmaine in the tennis club. Those present included Sheila Endwhistle and Chief Superintendent Charles Morrow, seated in the second row, who discreetly played footsie together. Sheila, as a wedding planner, had given Charmaine some advice about the afters. Geoffrey Brewer, Douglas's accountant, whose arm was in a sling, sat beside the canoodling amateur podiatrists. Excessive public arm wrestling had resulted in serious ligament damage. Desiree Honeycombe, the bride's hairdresser, sat in the third row beside Marius Mountmartin and made a silent promise to take up tennis. Behind them sat Joshua Shoshowski, who occasionally tracked down the disappeared who owed money to the bank and who was disappointed to discover that Geoffrey's arm-wrestling companion was absent. Joshua had a soft spot for Douglas, who he regarded as frequently linguistically confused. Whenever he was employed by Douglas he was always informed the work related to a distressed account of a disappeared debtor. In his experience it wasn't the bank account that was distressed but the disappeared who owed the bank money when he discovered their whereabouts. Beside him sat Dr Norman Zendlove, who regularly went on weekend walks with Douglas and occasionally referred distraught patients in trouble to Cyril for legal advice. Beside the good doctor sat a fierce looking Miranda Braithwaite who because she had arrived a little late didn't want to make a fuss joining Cyril in the front row. Her enraged focus was on Desiree Honeycombe, who seemed intent on pressing up as close as possible to Marius Mountmartin, who sat rooted to his seat, despite enough spare room along the row to seat at least four others.

Charmaine was anxious to ensure that the church, mostly used for pre or post funeral services, was cheerfully and colourfully decorated to mark her second attempt at a big day. Flowers ordered from Oxton's premier florist shop, 'Tulips Charms', were spread around the church walls. Unfortunately, Tulip Brown, the owner, had taken ill the night before the wedding and the flowers had been organised and delivered by her assistant of six weeks, Gladys Rose. Unexpectedly, communications between boss and assistant got confused and instead of delivering and laying out ten large wedding-style flower arrangements at the front and sides of the church Gladys had incongruously dressed the church with ten oversized wreaths. She had wrongly assumed the reference to a wedding in her written instructions was mistaken and that the only ceremonies that took place in the cemetery church related to the recently deceased and funerals.

Douglas, who had left the flower arrangements to Charmaine to organise, regarded the presence of so many wreaths as ominous but said nothing. Charmaine, who was enraged, said nothing as she didn't want to delay the ceremony and being recognised as Douglas's lawfully wedded wife. As far as she was concerned, she was going to ensure that the decorative wreaths resulted in Gladys Rose's career as a florist never blossoming and her employment by Tulip rapidly terminated, or as she later colourfully told Douglas, 'She's fuckin dead and buried, mon.' As their marriage ceremony had been celebrated in the cemetery's church, this sentiment was regarded by Douglas as totally appropriate.

The atmosphere in the church was not helped by the presence of a coffin behind the rector, poorly covered by a blanket, containing the body of Arthur Lamb, the towns oldest butcher who had died two days earlier. His funeral was scheduled to take place an hour after the wedding and the undertakers, getting the timing wrong, had delivered the coffin too early to the church, just before the happy couple and the wedding guests arrived. The presence of Arthur's remains in the church was a notable first for Oxton Town. The town's records, going back centuries, disclosed no previous church wedding attended by a dead person.

Everyone suitably seated, the ceremony got under way.

'We are gathered here today to celebrate the life of Charmaine and Arthur... er... the wedding of Charmaine and Douglas,' commenced a clearly flustered Rector Peter Howick.

'Not for many years have we celebrated a funeral... er... a

wedding in this house of God and I welcome you all here for what is a special day. It is joyous to have before me two people so alive... er... so alive in love, eager to bury, er sorry, to tie the knot of matrimony until upon death they do depart.'

'They will be back here then,' shouted Dr Norman Zendlove, who had before leaving home, because it was his day off and he had nothing better to do beforehand, lowered three large glasses of sherry.

'Shush,' uttered Sheila spontaneously, assuming the role of marriage planner in charge.

'Douglas we all know as one of Oxton's most upstanding citizens. In all his banking activities he is a debit... er a credit to his sadly recently deceased mother, Betty. Although buried just a couple of hundred yards away, I know she is here in the church with us, not in body but in spirit.'

The rector hesitated and took a nervous glance over his shoulder at the departed butcher's coffin, wondering should his presence also be acknowledged. Deciding no, he continued

'Douglas has asked me to share with you his wish that at the end of our ceremony we all gather around Betty's grave so that she is truly part of our celebration today.'

'Charmaine is new to our parish. In her short time in Oxton she has become a valued member of our community and made her presence felt.'

'Leave sex out of it,' shouted Norman Zendlove from the aisles to more shushes.

'And now for the formalities,' announced the rector.

'Do you, Douglas Beechcroft, take Charmaine Lloyd as your lawful wedded wife, from this day forth, to love and to cherish, through sick and thin, oops sorry, sorry, through thick and sin... er thick and thin, until death you do depart according to God's holy ordinances?'

'I do,' responded Douglas

'Do you, Charmaine Lloyd, take Douglas Beechcroft as your lawful wooded, er... sorry... your lawful wedded husband, from this day forth, to love and to cherish through, er... thick and thin, until death you do depart according to God's co-ordinates... oh dear... holy ordinances?'

'I do,' responded Charmaine with a sigh of relief.

'As the sacred cows... er vows have been exchanged I now pronounce you man and wife.'

Then to a burst of applause and shouts of congratulations the bride and groom kissed. Buried in the noise of the congratulatory shouts was Norman Zendlove's offer to milk the cows.

Ceremony over, the rector then led the assembled throng to the graveside of Douglas's mother. Unfortunately, in the excitement of the moment, upon the ceremony ending, a crucial announcement was omitted. Before those present exited the church, Peter Howick forgot to warn of the peril poised by the grave newly opened to receive Arthur Lamb's remains adjacent to the plot in which Douglas's mother, Betty, was buried.

'And now let me introduce Douglas to say a few words,' said the rector after everybody had gathered around Betty's grave.

'You don't have to, we already know him,' shouted the unusually voluble inebriated psychiatrist. This time there were no shushes and the gravesiders just laughed.

Standing in front of his deceased mother's headstone, an emotional Douglas spoke. 'Mum, you spent many years urging me to find the right woman to marry. I want you to be part of this day, the happiest day of my life. So here we are and here with me is my beautiful wife Charmaine. I know we have your blessing, Mum, and may you rest in peace.'

There was a moment's silence and then applause. Desiree Honeycombe, who had for about nine years been Betty's hairdresser, started to cry and leant into Marius Mountmartin standing beside her for comfort. Marius, who was being stared at by Miranda, not anticipating the accident-prone hairdresser's need to be up close and personal, stepped backwards and instantly disappeared, falling into Arthur Lamb's open grave. Desiree screamed as everyone, aghast, stared down into the grave.

Charlie Chuckles shouted, 'Are you all right?'

'I think so,' replied the fallen tennis coach, 'nothing broken.'

Charlie bent down over the grave saying, 'Take my hand.'

Marius obeyed orders, reached up and grabbed on to Charlie's hand. Charlie started to pull to help Marius climb back out. Unfortunately, just as Marius's head appeared above ground the loose soil around the grave gave way and the clown fell headfirst into the grave on top of Marius, unintentionally breaking his arm. A similar performance in the circus ring, Cyril realised, would have elicited shrieks of laughter and wild applause. It just seemed a little out of place as the last act at a wedding ceremony held in Oxton's cemetery.

An hour later, as the newlyweds and their guests sat down to a dinner of roast beef and Yorkshire pudding in the Ancient Wig, Marius Mountmartin exited Oxton Hospital's radiography department, having had his arm x-rayed, and was returned by wheelchair to accident and emergency. Miranda, who had volunteered to accompany him in the ambulance summoned by the rector, waited to take him to his home by taxi after his broken arm had been put in a plaster cast. Back at Charmaine and Douglas's afters, Desiree Honeycombe, sitting beside Cyril, turned to the lawyer, tentatively asking 'You're not going to sue me again, are you Mr Braithwaite?'

'No, Desiree,' Cyril replied with an audible sigh. 'Firstly, you didn't hit him with a brush, secondly, the grave digger should have placed something sturdy over the grave to prevent an accident and thirdly, it isn't your fault Mr Mountmartin broke his arm.' Cyril then somewhat ambiguously asserted, 'Clowns will be clowns and there's not much you or I can do about that,' and took a sip of his pint of ale.

Johnny Bleak, seated at the end of the same table, wasn't listening to the chatter all around him. Troubled by Charlie Chuckles' unexpected plunge into the grave opened for Arthur Lamb, he was in deep contemplation mulling over the wisdom of his employing a clown as the cemetery's assistant manager. The one positive was the discovery that a clown can emerge unscathed after tumbling into a grave. Perhaps, he reasoned, the rough and tumble of the circus ring provided great training for coping with the daily hazards involved in managing a cemetery.

41

THE MEETING THE next day took place in the New York style deli. Joshua believed it an appropriate place to complete his investigation, being the first location put under surveillance by him at its commencement. She was seated at a table by the window as cool as a cucumber displaying no signs of nervous tension when he arrived and introduced himself. He had previously recognised her from the photograph perched on Cyril's desk. At the previous day's wedding, as all the guests walked down to the graveside, he had suggested they meet up the next morning to discuss an issue of mutual interest.

Introductions over, Miranda instantly came to the point before Joshua could even raise it.

'You're the criminal turned private detective, aren't you?' Miranda more asserted than asked, immediately putting Joshua in his place. 'Cyril told me all about you last night. You're investigating the great letter writing mystery and you want to ask me all about it. Am I right?'

'Uh huh,' Joshua responded, nodding vigorously.

'Well, I've got nothing to say on that subject,' said Miranda emphatically and then went uncharacteristically quiet.

'Then why did you agree to meet me when I phoned you earlier this morning,' asked Joshua.

'I was curious. What do you know?' Miranda responded.

'Well, I think the anonymous correspondents are you and Ethel,' replied Joshua, not mentioning Ethel had already confessed.

'You think or you know?' queried Miranda, marshalling her family's traditional skill in the art of cross-examination.

'I think I know,' countered Joshua, applying his own extensive court room knowledge.

'Tell me more,' retorted Miranda.

'It's all quite simple really. You hate Bartholomew Bull because of the way you and Cyril were treated after your father's death and you wanted to exact revenge on him. You also wanted to exact revenge on all of those clients who contrived consultations with Cyril just to find out more about the circumstances relating to his death. You discussed it all with Ethel Edelwitz, who had a similar ambition and also wanted to deliver some payback. You both had lots of opportunities to plot when you met up at the tennis club. With Ethel's help you accessed the names and addresses of your victims and their spouses in Cyril's office. The fact that he always recorded the name of a client's partner or spouse on his laptop made the job easy. You and Ethel together made up spurious messages by cutting up stories published in the Oxton Daily News. Ethel then ensured that any letter recipient who sought Cyril's advice was redirected to Moore Bull & Co so they were stuck with a series of nonsensical cases. Pamela Bull was the only exception, as you wanted Cyril to give Bartholomew as much trouble as possible. Basically, you and Ethel cooked up a series of fake cases to cause various people maximum grief and to generate work and fees for Cyril. In doing so you chose to ignore the stress and upset you caused to the recipients of false allegations about their spouse's conduct. To you both they were just unavoidable collateral damage.'

Joshua waited for a reaction and remained tight lipped on the confrontation he had just an hour earlier with Ethel after calling to her home on her planned second day off work. She had spilled the beans in return for Joshua's promise to say nothing to anyone about her part in the plot, and in particular nothing to Cyril.

'That's a very interesting theory, Mr Shoshowski. You have proof of course?' she enquired.

'Well not exactly. In fact, if I am right I don't really want proof. Cyril, your husband, has been very good to me and if all of this comes out, he could get into awful difficulties. He could be disciplined and prevented from practising as a solicitor. I do want it all sorted though and I thought you might come up with something,' he explained helpfully.

Ten minutes later the get-together ended on a cordial note. Joshua departed, leaving Miranda thoughtfully masticating on her 'authentic' New York style crusty onion bagel filled with cream cheese which, unknown to Miranda, was a poor replica of the original Yiddisha New York production. As Cyril's growing proportions clearly illustrated, the only true exponent and producer of the original authentic bagel in Oxton Town was his receptionist cum secretary, Ethel Edelwitz. Unknown to Cyril one of the reasons for her taking a day off from the legal practice was that Ethel was moving house. What she had also forgotten to mention to Cyril was that it was his house, with Miranda's help, into which she was moving.

* * *

The sun peaked out from the side of the white giraffe-shaped cloud and spread its warm rays along the wall directly opposite the window in the office of the only living partner of the solicitor's firm of Braithwaite Marshall & Co. It was briefly eclipsed by the giraffe's nose before it reappeared and decided that those beneath it deserved to benefit from its warm glow until nightfall came. It ordered the remaining clouds floating past to avoid its path to allow it to shine uninterrupted until it was forced to sink slowly out of sight to be replaced at nightfall by a flamboyant full moon celebrating the middle of a month in the Jewish calendar. The sun wondered why the middle of a Jewish month always coincided with a full moon whilst the middle of a Christian month only occasionally did so. And why, it mused, are all Christian years of twelve-month duration with a leap year containing an additional day every four years, whilst Jewish years are of twelve-month duration with a leap year of an additional month added seven times in every nineteen-year cycle? Perhaps, it concluded from a solar perspective, Jewish people are more enthusiastic leapers than Christians or maybe they just enjoy complicating the number of months required to record the passing of a full year. Likely, it believed, it was all explained in the Talmud which one day it hoped to study.

The rubber tree, still untouched by Ethel's threatened pruning, relaxed contentedly in the sunshine and marvelled at how its branches and leaves had filled most of the spare space across a third of Cyril's office. It flexed its roots in the new all-purpose seed and potting compost in which they had been buried by Cyril. It then fed off the new multipurpose Miracle-Gro bio-stimulant all-purpose plant food Cyril had fed to it earlier that day to ensure it would keep its pecker up, as he had previously somewhat indelicately informed Ethel.

The Swiss cheese plant, re-potted and also fed Miracle-Gro, hung precariously over the side of the fireplace resenting that once again the warmth of the day was reflecting off its vegetating companion while it sat in the dark shadows of the raised roller blinds. It was determined to grow its way across the room and to ultimately raise its leaves directly in front of the rubber tree to bask in the warmth of the early afternoon sun.

It was unusually quiet for 3 p.m. on a Thursday afternoon. The phone rang but no one replied. Ethel Edelwitz had taken another day off and Cyril was in the Ancient Wig animatedly discussing with Chief Superintendent Charles Morrow whether a clown who struck his wife in the face with a custard pie at her request could be arrested and prosecuted for assault. They then moved on to consider if the answer was yes whether she could be prosecuted as an accomplice to or for inciting a criminal act and whether he might be found not guilty due to duress. Whether a custard pie could be categorised as a dangerous weapon was a conundrum of greater complexity. Both bored with ale, a full bottle of Jameson's Black Barrel Irish Whiskey, accompanied by a jug of water and bucket of ice, was ordered. Various toasts were proposed in tribute to the continuing unexpected success of Oxton Rovers, who had won their third match in succession and were sitting on the top of their league table. Fortunately, as the brains of two of Oxton Town's leading citizens were enveloped in an alcoholic haze, no major criminal act nor urgent legal dispute occurred that required the attention of either.

Just after 3.30 p.m., having confirmed Cyril's whereabouts by discreetly glancing into the Ancient Wig, Miranda entered Cyril's office, greeting the rubber tree with a cheery 'hello'. Envelopes speedily addressed were filled with an identical letter, which she first photocopied. It read

YOU HAVE BEEN THE VICTIM OF A HOAX.

IGNORE ANONYMOUS ALLEGATIONS PREVIOUSLY MADE.

SORRY FOR ALL THE BOTHER.

YOU WILL NOT HEAR FROM ME AGAIN THANKS TO MR SHOSHOWSKI.

ENJOY THE REST OF YOUR LIFE.

FROM YOUR SECRET FRIEND.

Unlike its predecessors the original letter had been typed and printed by Miranda on a PC available for confidential public use in Oxton Library. Once printed it had been instantly deleted. She had used the same PC to address envelope labels.

Miranda was sticking to her side of the bargain and trusted Joshua would stick to his. She had agreed to mention his name in the letter to ensure no one queried the fees charged by him, Bartholomew Bull, Cyril or any other firm of solicitors who represented the embattled spouses who were the victims of her and Ethel's little charade. She reckoned she had by now exacted sufficient revenge on the clients revealed by Ethel as featuring in the FILS online file as a result of their prurient inquiries about her father's death and on Bartholomew Bull for his mistreatment of her, Cyril and Ethel. The game was now over. She now had her

Marius and Ethel, with Miranda's blessing, was about to get what she wanted.

Meanwhile, the person on Ethel's Wanted List remained blissfully unaware of what was in store as he lowered his fourth glass of Jameson on the rocks and proposed a toast to Sheila Endwhistle, interrupting an ebullient Charles Morrow as he slurringly detailed the music he and Sheila had chosen for their planned registry office wedding and described the likely afters. Anxious to impress her betrothed with her professionalism as a wedding planner, Sheila had rapidly put everything in motion.

Despite Charles' inebriated condition Cyril successfully limited his description of afters to the post ceremony dinner and speeches and curtailed the chief superintendent's enthusiastic attempt to pictorially depict his much-anticipated post nuptial celebratory intimate engagement with Sheila on the night of their wedding. He also resisted the temptation to try and persuade the chief super that he should carry on Douglas Beechcroft's innovation and deliver a speech at the grave of his deceased mother, Maude, immediately after the ceremony. As far as Cyril was concerned, he had had his fill of cemeteries.

42

IT WAS MIDNIGHT when Cyril tottered drunkenly up the path of 43 Larkspur Grove. He was relieved to find the house in pitch darkness, believing that meant that Miranda was fast asleep recovering from her tennis and aerobic endeavours. The door seemed to move from side to side as he slowly inserted his key in the lock and carefully pushed it open, anxious to not awake Miranda from her slumbers.

Entering the hallway he made straight for the stairs, quietly undressing when he arrived at the top. Folding his clothes over a banister he carefully opened the bedroom door, crawled unannounced towards the bed, gently lifted the duvet, climbed in and let the duvet fall around him. He then instantly ended his association with the conscious world.

Cyril dreamt he was lying paralysed on a bed similar to his own being sexually assaulted by a woman who looked remarkably like Ethel Edelwitz, except she had long flowing hair which fell down to her shoulders and appeared a great deal more attractive.

He subconsciously wondered should he try to wake himself up but the touch of his dream-constructed companion felt far too good to interrupt. Suddenly it dawned on him, through an alcohol-induced somnolent haze, that he was reaching a crescendo reminiscent of a teenage wet dream that still featured in the top ten of Cyril's best remembered lifetime experiences. As he exploded in silent salute to nocturnal virtual reality, he acknowledged that Jameson's Black Barrel is a really superior blend of whiskey. It undoubtedly supplied the helping hand to its grateful imbibers Cyril had for so many years been seeking.

Cyril rolled over into a foetal position and fell into a deeper sleep. Lying beside him in the dark Ethel Edelwitz sighed contentedly. Despite the pitch black of the room, she now knew that Cyril was sculptured as she hoped and as her mother desired. Despite the Jameson's his body rhythm linked to her aerobic gyrations had proved just right. On their first night to make love they had struck the jackpot and come together. Ethel felt that in the lottery of life she had finally got hold of a winning ticket. Her move that afternoon into Larkspur Grove together with all her previously packed belongings was destined to work out fine.

Ethel's first objective had been accomplished. Clearly, Cyril's penis did not have to be reconfigured. She would not know whether she had achieved her second objective for between five to six weeks. At least now there was a reasonable possibility a little Braithwitz would come into the world. As for her third objective, that of turning Cyril into a millionaire, it remained a project to work on. Tomorrow would be another day and she knew there would be a lot of explaining to do. Turning over she cuddled into Cyril's back, threw her left arm over his shoulder and fell sound asleep.

* * *

In the kitchen Miranda's note to Cyril explaining her unexpected departure with Aloysius to Marius Mountmartin's country cottage remained pinned to the kitchen notice board unread.

* * *

In Oxton Hospital Pamela Bull slept fitfully, locked into a bizarre nightmare in which she was the victim of repetitive physical assaults by live mobile marauding black conveyor belt flaps which had invaded Oxton Town from some unknown galaxy and enslaved its inhabitants. The results of tests undertaken to ascertain whether she had yet fully recovered from concussion were awaited.

* * *

In Dorchester Avenue Hilda Hessleberg sat peacefully on her lounge room couch knitting a woollen jumper, which she intended to give as a gift to Geoffrey Brewer to thank him for their lunchtime daily jousts in the Ancient Wig. In Finsbury Court, sitting up in bed, Geoffrey Brewer for the umpteenth time repetitively apologised and promised a still livid Jocelyn there would be no more public arm wrestling in the New York deli. Having made Geoffrey grovel for almost an hour, she called him an idiot, told him to switch off the light, shut up, wrap around her bottom and go to sleep.

* * *

In Oxton Woods, perched once again in the old oak tree, Joshua Shoshowski, using a specially designed night vision camera, filmed for posterity a very drunk chief superintendent thrashing about with Sheila Endwhistle in his Jaguar sports car – a useful piece of filmed insurance to provide some bargaining power should Joshua have any future brushes with the law. Despite the couple being free to play in the chief superintendent's home, they had chosen their familiar woodside location to celebrate the start of their new life together.

* * *

In Chester Avenue, Fred Endwhistle sat up happily in bed watching an episode of Law and Order munching cheese and onion crisps and slurping a large mug of hot chocolate. Without warning, a fart as loud as a clap of thunder echoed throughout the room. Fred looked sheepishly around and then remembered he was alone. No one shouted abuse or struck him violently across the back of his head. Thanks to Chief Superintendent Charles Morrow law and order prevailed. Fred lifted the bed covers, took a deep sniff, wiggled his nostrils and belched contentedly.

* * *

A serene Judge Gerard Podge sat up in bed. He had just finished being bottle-fed his nightly hot milk by Lily. He held lovingly onto a new five foot teddy bear that he had purchased online just two weeks earlier as he sucked on a baby soother. After receipt by him of Cyril Braithwaite's letter approved by Lily, she had moved into a spare bedroom and announced she would not again sleep with him until he got some psychiatric help. Next Wednesday they were both due at a consultation with Dr Norman Zendlove, who had only recently recovered from a painful hernia operation. The judge was looking forward to getting the good doctor to persuade Lily they could both have so much more fun together if she purchased and wore every night a pink babygro on sale on the same website from which he had acquired his blue and green babygros. If she agreed to do so he knew everything would then be fine between them both and Braithwaite's role in their lives would be rendered obsolete. He was looking forward to dressing Lily in a nappy.

* * *

Johnny Bleak sat in his lounge room rocking chair watching a late-night repeat of the movie Four Weddings and a Funeral. He had seen it eighteen times previously on TV. He especially loved the movie's depiction of a funeral. Despite his austere demeanour Johnny enjoyed nothing better than a good belly laugh. Maybe, he thought, employing a clown as his assistant manager at Oxton Cemetery will lighten the mood at future burials, put the bereaved in better humour and give them all a laugh. Provided, of course, the clown doesn't habitually fall into graves opened to accommodate the latest deceased. He was considering asking his newly appointed assistant manager, who had reverted to the name of Alphonse Smiley and had that morning resigned from the circus, to dress and make up as a clown again for the town's next funeral to gauge people's reaction. He thought that could be really interesting!

* * *

In Oxton Manor, Charmaine and Douglas Beechcroft lay in bed repetitively playing on their television screen the footage taken at their wedding of a clown falling headfirst into a grave on top of Marius Mountmartin as tears of laughter ran down their cheeks. 'I hope that my mum enjoyed the entertainment,' remarked

Douglas. 'Such a great idea, part of our wedding in a cemetery. Didn't expect the cemetery to provide Charlie Chuckles as an added extra though. You couldn't predict that one. Life really is a lottery. It really is strange the way stuff happens.'

'Sure is,' replied Charmaine suddenly feeling exhausted. She partially sat up, reached over, kissed Douglas on the cheek, then lay down on her back and, still smiling, fell fast asleep.